Gorilla With Cellulite

Believe in Life's Magic

Rosaria La Pietra

BALBOA.
PRESS

A DIVISION OF HAY HOUSE

Balboa Press books may be ordered through booksellers or by contacting:

Balboa Press
A Division of Hay House
1663 Liberty Drive
Bloomington, IN 47403
www.balboapress.com
1 (877) 407-4847

Because of the dynamic nature of the Internet, any web addresses or links contained in this book may have changed since publication and may no longer be valid. The views expressed in this work are solely those of the author and do not necessarily reflect the views of the publisher, and the publisher hereby disclaims any responsibility for them.

The author of this book does not dispense medical advice or prescribe the use of any technique as a form of treatment for physical, emotional, or medical problems without the advice of a physician, either directly or indirectly. The intent of the author is only to offer information of a general nature to help you in your quest for emotional and spiritual well-being. In the event you use any of the information in this book for yourself, which is your constitutional right, the author and the publisher assume no responsibility for your actions.

Any people depicted in stock imagery provided by Thinkstock are models, and such images are being used for illustrative purposes only. Certain stock imagery © Thinkstock.

Print information available on the last page.

ISBN: 978-1-5043-5758-6 (sc)
ISBN: 978-1-5043-5759-3 (hc)
ISBN: 978-1-5043-5760-9 (e)

Library of Congress Control Number: 2017902809

Balboa Press rev. date: 03/16/2017

Introduction

The Mission of this book is to inspire, entertain you and hopefully to help you see how magical your life is.

I started to see the magic in my life when I started reading my first self development book "Listen to Your Body, Your best friend on Earth" by Lise Bourbeau. Before getting acquainted with Lise, I had a pretty negative look on life, I disliked my body, went on crazy diets, drunk a lot of alcohol, hated my job and my romantic relationships were disastrous. I honestly believed that I was born unlucky and that good things happened to other people. How could I deserve happiness when I was not slim enough, pretty enough, rich enough and somehow I got dumped by all the boys I fell for? I used to take refuge in romantic novels and films, they cheered me up and kept me hopeful that one day I would meet the love of my life and that I would have my happily ever after.

Several self development books, yoga courses, spirituality workshops, tons of self observation, I finally understand that I am fully responsible of how I feel everyday and everyday I can make a choice to think and feel miserable or think and feel good about myself and my circumstances. I finally learnt what love, forgiveness and gratitude mean and I strive to put them into practice everyday.

Along this journey, I decided that I wanted to inspire others who are going through the same issues that blocked my happiness. From there my idea to combine spirituality and romantic novels was born, 'Gorilla with Cellulite' was born.

Happy reading

Contents

PART 1

In the beginning there was an Ape

Dear Mac

Today is the first day of my new life! This morning the book was finally delivered to the office! Oh I love Amazon . . . it is so reliable, unlike all men I know!

Anyway, let's not go there! They are absolutely useless . . .

So I was saying, the book has arrived. Mum suggested I read it, 'Listen to Your Body, your best friend on Earth'. My mother is and always was a bit out there, very New Age! But I am in such a downward spiral at the moment, nothing is working out for me, I figured I have nothing to lose but £12 on a book!

I can positively say that I have not been happy in a very long time and not to be a drama queen, I can't even remember when I truly felt happy! When things go well for me I know that something bad is going to happen! My lovely flatmates Jamie and Millie are in the same situation and just last Friday we promised each other, on yet another boozy night, that we were going to seek something to get us out of this funk! Jamie said he will take up yoga (I personally think he should take up a personal trainer, cos he could do with losing a little weight!) I love him and I don't want him to get a heart attack, his belly looks like a baby bump of a 5 month pregnant woman! Millie said that she will look into a holiday for us in Ibiza, maybe for the end of June to celebrate my birthday. She seems to think that we need a holiday! Drinking and partying in the sun, maybe she has a point. My parents live in Ibiza and if we went we could stay with them. But then again, what if, for some reason (very unlikely reason) I manage to meet a boy? I would not want to bring him to my parents' place! Anyway, let's see, Millie comes up with amazing ideas when she's had a few, but nothing ever comes of them as she is permanently working.

I have decided to listen to my Mum for once and take up her advice. She says that things are great for me and that I should be grateful for who I am and what I am. I should count my blessings. What blessings I say?! She always says "Honey you are a beautiful, smart, successful young lady and have a lot going on for you... you just need to see it!" But as far as my eyes and head can see, I am none of that! And I feel that things have hit rock bottom!

Hang on, actually things did get worse ...this morning... I had a meeting with Chris, the HOT junior office manager. We went to the boardroom, which has such incredibly unattractive lighting, and as I sat down my skirt zip broke, making a sort of fart sound! It was so embarrassing. I am sure that he heard the noise, but I pretended that nothing happened. I cleared my throat and opened up my folder, very aware of how red my cheeks had gone and swiftly moved into the agenda for the day. I felt like Hell had opened up and swallowed me, why did my big fat arse have to do that to me in front of Chris!

Oh Mac, have I told you about Chris (I know, you think "only once or twice....")? He is just so hoot/good looking/handsome. You name it! Mmmmm he's like Brad Pitt's younger, fitter brother. I know in my heart that he is the man for me. I'm surprised I don't drool at my desk when I see him walk through the office!

He looked super cute this morning! I could barely take my eyes off him(when he wasn't looking at me naturally! I can't meet his eyes, I get too flustered and I am afraid I might blurt out something silly like 'you are so gorgeous, I love you!') He has the most amazing, penetrating blue eyes! He must think I am a loser. Well he is right, I am! Although my Mum doesn't think so but she is my Mother after all!

So, my efforts on becoming thinner and therefore less of a loser are failing... I cannot believe that the Cambridge diet has not worked, it worked for Vicky (my assistant), and why after all these efforts I am still a size 12! I give up, what's the point; I put myself through so much torture and for what? So that my big fat behind explodes in my skirt in front of the delicious Chris?

Thank God for Vicky though, when I finished the meeting, I asked Chris to leave and called her into the boardroom and she helped me fix the skirt with a pin. What a way to start a Monday and I had been looking forward to having a private meeting with Chris for such a long time! I even had a dream about him. We were in a park, having a picnic, we were drinking champagne, eating strawberries, and he leant over and said: "I want to kiss you! I love you so much, I must have you!" and just as he was kissing me, the alarm went off! Arrrgh!!!! Annoying.... But such a lovely dream... ... ..

After the meeting, the book arrived . . . I took it as a sign . . . You know how much I believe in signs. Could this book help me to change my life? Is it yet another self-help book that my Mum has suggested I read? I love my Mum, of course I do, but sometimes I think she is from another planet. Positive-thinking, vegan diet, yoga, meditation, self-love . . . she is like Mother Teresa, yet she ended up with such a mess of a daughter! Maybe it's her soul mission, she always harps on about soul mission. I mean, what on earth is that? Who knows, I have never asked her as I don't want to get her started on the cosmic/astrology/spiritual bla, bla, bla ....

The foreword of this book says *"This Book has been written especially for you"*, what? - a loser like me??? *"By venturing into its pages, you have consciously made a decision to improve the quality of your life"* So far so good… *"For whatever reason you opened this book"* – Er because I want Chris to be my boyfriend, I want to be skinny and I hate my job with a passion! *"Be assured that throughout its pages you and I will become friends on your journey of transformation… Hopefully, you have chosen to read this book because you've made the valuable decision to finally become the master of your life"* Yes I want to start . . . Chris you and I *will* get married! It *will* be on a white, sandy beach in Thailand, I *will* be wearing a white dress and I *will* be a beautiful size 8. Daydreaming, my favourite pastime… … … … …

Oh shit, it's gone midnight, I really need to get myself to sleep… I am feeling hopeful!

Good Night Mac!

K x

Wednesday, 6th May 6.30 am

Dear Mac

OMG, WTF! What happened to me during the night? I woke up looking like a big hairy She-gorilla, (need to book my wax today)! God I am so fat! My thighs jiggle when I move and look like cottage cheese. Honestly I must stop eating the stuff – they say "you are what you eat" – seemingly I am a tub of lumpy dairy. From today I am going to be super-healthy! No food today!

Best get ready and get to work. . I need to make look myself presentable, although I will definitely stay out Chris' way today . . . I am still so embarrassed to face him. Nonetheless I do feel hopeful this morning, this could truly be the first day of my new life!

10.30 pm

Hey Mac - What a day! . . . it felt sooo long . . . paperwork, silly meetings, boooring... HR is not for me, office politics are not for me! I did see Chris, we met in the lift after work. As per usual when I see him I go into a fluster, I was so embarrassed from the zip/skirt-breaking incident, I could not bring myself to string a single sentence together, I only managed a "Hi". He looked amazing. I love his thick, dark blond hair, blue eyes and he is so fiiiit.... I think he plays rugby, I love rugby players... and he smells divine... oh I sooo love him, I can just visualise our beach wedding; he is wearing a white linen suit, no shirt . . .

Yes! I must lose weight to get Chris! I have been good all day, ate absolutely nothing, just drunk plenty of coffee and sugar free red bull to keep me going and then tonight I blew it! Jamie and Millie ordered a pizza takeaway and I could not resist, there was ice cream too! I don't know how many calories I ate, but I don't feel so good right now. Will I ever learn? I will start again tomorrow, as Scarlet O'Hara says "after all tomorrow is another day" That's my motto!

Anyhow, let's draw a thick, bold, dark line under that! On a more positive note Mac, I have started reading dear Mother's book and, I have decided, I am going to keep a very open mind and even do the exercises that Lise suggests doing at the end of each chapter! I always swore not to get sucked into these so called "Self Help"

Books, they are silly! Look at Vicky, my assistant, she reads tonnes of them and she is still the same! But at my age, I just feel that I don't want to carry on like this. I am desperate, I am 29, fat, single and I hate my job! I want to get married (maybe to Chris!), I want a new job, I want to be slim . . . so as the X Factor competitors say "this could be my last chance"!

So anyway . . . Chapter 1 is entitled "A common Purpose." Here are the main points I picked up.....

"Have you ever stopped to ask yourself what you are doing on the planet? Why are you here? What is your purpose? The answer is simple . . . TO EVOLVE, TO GROW. We are here to grow as individuals and grow collectively." Maybe she is talking about evolution of the species?

"As manifestations of Universal Energy, as living things, once we stop growing, we die. . . As human beings, full expression of our growth happens on a soul level. The seed of the Divine Life Force is planted in the soul of every human being, thus our sole purpose is our 'soul purpose'.

In every religion, the fundamental truths are LOVE and FAITH. Being human, we become entangled in our problems" - You can say that again! *'Complicating our lives'* me? Noooo! *"Throwing ourselves off the path and losing touch with the two simple truths. Jesus taught us that unconditional love for ourselves and for each other is the light that will keep our vision clear, allowing us to clearly see our path in life. Once a human being has learned to love himself and others unconditionally he will have mastered the material works and found inner peace and true fulfilment. We are all manifestations of God's pure love and energy."*

Jeez Louise! She sounds like Mum, the New Age basher!! But as I said, although I want to throw up in my mouth after reading this first chapter, I am determined to do the exercises; my desire for a better life is stronger than my scepticism. I want Chris, I want to be slim and I want to be like Stephanie! Oh, have I mentioned her before? - Miss Picture Perfect. French - well she says she is Parisian (excuse me!)- tall, dark long hair, slim (of course, all French women are slim!), wealthy (of bloody course!) and engaged to Paul. Who is also perfect! Although I have actually never seen him, I just overheard her talk about him on the phone. Tall, good looking, dark and intense, wealthy! Yes she has it all. No wonder there is nothing left for me! Stephanie makes me feel so self-conscious, I always seem to stuff my face after an encounter with her! She is like a race horse and I am a she-gorilla with orange-peel thighs! The b***h has NO cellulite, how is it possible?!!! You may wonder how I know she has no cellulite? I have seen her in a biking last year, during our company day. Our boss gave treated us to a SPA day, naturally I was in my bathrobe all day. I mean …I am not going to be the joke of the company and wear a bikini in fort of everyone? Mind you, I am already the joke of the company! Ahhh self-pity, self-pity!

BTW I think gorillas are amazing animals, but it is not very attractive for a woman of the human species to look like a gorilla!

As usual, I have gone off-track, let's get back to Lise.

"Remember that the Earth itself is a living entity. In Quantum Theory, we are tied to the Earth and to each other on a cellular level. Physicists have known for many years that energy is indestructible and boundless. Our energy field, or life force, is interchangeable with everything and everyone around us, just as other fields interact with ours. In taking personal responsibility for our spiritual growth, we contribute to the

growth of other and the growth and harmony of our own planet." Wow - *tooo* far-out for me at this stage!

"Throughout this book, you will be given tools that will help you become the MASTER OF YOUR LIFE", Ok now she is making sense again "As you develop faith and love of yourself, you will radiate a powerful, positive energy that will transform everyone and *everything* around you." That's great, but really I am just looking at improving my life. Leave saving the world to Mum, Greenpeace and Amnesty International.

"You must take your eyes off what is happening outside of you and take a moment to look inwards." Whatever that means Mac?! *"I know you are telling yourself 'it sounds so easy, but I find it very difficult to look inside myself. I am afraid of what I might find.' This fear has been programmed in your subconscious mind from past experiences on the material level, from your parents and from society in general."* It is always the parent's fault! *"The point is, it has been programmed in and has undermined the state of bliss that we are born into naturally. The universe creates us in happiness and love... IT IS OUR NATURAL STATE TO BE HAPPY AND TO GROW BY VIRTUE OF BEING ALIVE"*

Ergo Mac, I need to start looking inside myself and there I will meet the divinity that resides in me. And how the hell do I start looking inside? Divinity what? I feel as though she is talking a different language. And it all sounds quite ridiculous! But I promised I would not be cynical about it and give it a chance.

"Do not be afraid to look inside yourself – you will find your inner power (which we will refer as your inner God from now on). Only by finding Him and befriending Him will you have all the strength you will need

to accomplish what it is you desire, become the master of your own life."
Why does she refer to God as male, I think it is wrong!

"If you are a beginner of the path to personal growth, you may experience some distress and some discomfort on the physical and emotional level. You might have the impression that your very foundation is crumbling as you let go of your old programming. It is only an illusion. You are ridding yourself of the shackles of the past – letting go of emotional baggage and preconceived ideas. YOU ARE BECOMING FREE! Once you learn to trust, to have faith in the process, you will let go of the fear and learn to love... YOU MUST ACT! Only through conscious action and repetition will you achieve your goals, intensifying your purification and growth. Remember, you are REPROGRAMMING your subconscious mind. The subconscious mind only understands ACTION. ... remain MINDFUL and understand that the only reality there is, exists in the inner realm. All else is illusion. Before becoming visible, everything is created in the invisible."

Thus I am the way that I am because of some programming I picked up whilst growing up. What I now need to do is to re-programme my subconscious mind to change. Let go of the old me and welcome a new, improved version of me (?). Perhaps Apple could invent a software for humans to reprogram their sorry lives and become successful. If only Steve Jobs were alive! He could make it happen!

In addition to that I also need to BELIEVE and have FAITH.

"The only reason why you have not accomplished what you have wanted in your life thus far is because you did not BELIEVE it was possible. You did not have FAITH. One of the greatest mistakes we make as human beings is failing to accept this power. REMEMBER, thoughts are energy! Once your thoughts are clear, you will be able to manifest it, to create whatever you want."

A little too good to be true, but why not try? In for a penny, in for a pound. I once read a quote from Albert Einstein that says *'The definition of insanity: doing the same thing over and over again and expect different results'*. Mr Einstein had a point, so I will do something different for once in my life and I will give the exercises at the end of each chapter a go.

Chapter 1 Exercises:

>>*"Take a sheet of paper"* How old is Lise? Does anybody still use paper? I have my fabulous Mac *"..and write down everything you can remember doing IN THE PAST WEEK in the following categories:*

>>*What have you done just for yourself and made you feel good or brought you happiness?"*

Chocolate! I eat chocolate every day (apart from today, ha no, that's a lie, I had chocolate Chip ice cream!!) and it made me feel good, for 1 minute! Not much else I am afraid!

Wait, I forgot my best friends Jamie and Millie. Thank goodness for those two, they keep me sane and they love me just as I am. It's nice to be loved unconditionally, no judgment.

Jamie reminds me of a chocolate brown Labrador, he has gorgeous, big, brown eyes, brown hair and tall, but sadly he is a "little" (about 2 stone) overweight and his skin is very blemished. But he is an amazing, caring person and I wish I was attracted to him, but the thought of kissing him, nah... Chris, on the other hand... I am obsessed with him! He looks like a young Robert Redford... his voice is so deep oh... I have to stop, I am getting too excited and it's late, I might not be able to get to sleep!

Jamie is also very clever and artistic. He's the IT manager of a big American law firm (the same company Millie works for as a lawyer), but his true passion is photography. He takes fantastic pictures. He took a portrait picture of me and it has now become my profile picture on Facebook. I really don't like having my pictures taken, but this one shows me in a completely different light, I look stunning even if I say so myself!

As for Millie, she is actually American, from NYC. She is super smart, she is a lawyer. Millie and Jamie met when she started working for the firm. I have known Jamie since Uni, Manchester University to be precise. Yeah I know, not too shabby! We met in the student union one night during a battle of the bands gig. I was in love with this base player…. I know, know, I am your typical girl who wants to get together with the boy in a band. I am such a cliché!

Anyway, I think Millie is stunningly good-looking, she gets so much attention from men. When you look at her, you'd think she has it all, but she doesn't believe it! She is very hard on herself. I think she is perfect, skinny, big boobs, long, blond hair, green eyes and she has an investment banker boyfriend Marco! That boy is besotted with her and I think a proposal is on the cards!

Let's not get side-tracked though; these exercises are about me and my personal development! I can hear my Mum's voice "you are just as beautiful as Millie, you just have to believe it." Keep eating your quinoa and Kale Mum! She is crazy about Kale! She even wears t-shirt with word Kale written on them. I mean come on! She offered to buy me one… can you imagine, she is mental!

>>*List everyone who said or did something that made you feel criticised or judged. Then make a list of the situations in which you found*

yourself criticising or judging others. How did you feel? Do you see the relationship between the two?

Easy! My boss criticises me all the time! I never do anything right! He is a dick! and I judge him for being a dick, I guess?! How do I feel? Useless, angry, upset, anxious, I hate my job so much! The relationship between us two? Non-existent! It is strictly professional. I avoid him like the Plague, I mostly communicate with him by e-mail. I can't stand to be in the same room as him.

>>Repeat the following affirmation whenever you are alone with our thoughts until you feel you have accepted and let go of the above situation. Then go to chapter 2

I AM A MANIFESTATION OF THE DIVINE, I AM GOD AND I CREATE WHATEVER I DESIRE. KNOWING THIS, I FEEL A GREAT INNER STRENGTH AND A PROFOUND INNER PEACE.

Slim Body!

New job! Although I don't know what I want to do instead!

CHRIS mmmmmm ! I loooooove Him!

That's if from me, goodnight Mac, I am going to put you on charge, you are running low on batteries! (and me too!)

K x

Dear Mac,

Good evening,

I have done my homework and I have repeated the affirmation so many times, but I still feel the same. I guess I don't yet believe the words, but I remain hopeful. Hope is all I got! I just heard the words in my head, I am starting to sound like somebody on a reality TV competition!

My day was as sort of uneventful and painful as always. I had another embarrassing encounter with Chris! He came over to my desk to hand me some documents. Lord knows why, he has never come over to my desk, he generally drops all the paper work in Vicky's tray. In a very manly way, I must add! He kind of slams them on her desk, he is a rugby player after all, maybe his brain doesn't switch off from the game? I mean, maybe he day dreams like me? Anyway he looked like a movie star today! Just gorgeous. I was sipping on hot coffee and he said 'Good morning Kate, these are for you', I burnt my tongue, spilt coffee down my white blouse and a heart attack and went to heaven! I mumbled 'Thank you' without looking at him and thankfully he left me to my mess!!! I am so bashful when it comes to Chris. I know this sounds silly but when he looks at me I am afraid he can read my thoughts. "You look so good, I want to be your girlfriend, kiss me . . ." the rest I don't care to share with you Mac ;)

Come back to Earth Kate! I am always on Planet Romance when I think of Chris.

I took a full lunch hour today – I never take a full lunch hour, but from today I will dedicate it to reading the book and do the exercises. - I read chapter 2, "Whole Mind Integration", with great interest and the following are the best bits (I think!):

WARNING MAC. Some stuff might seem a little out there, but keep an open mind.

"Studies indicate that the average human being is 90% unconscious (only 10% conscious) of what they do, say, think and feel. ...We will try together to modify your state of unconsciousness because becoming aware of what we feel, think, say or do is instrumental in getting what we want out of life."

I definitely need to modify my unconscious mind.

"The SUBCONSCIOUS MIND is situated in the solar plexus region, between your heart and your navel. It is directly in tune with your emotional body. I am sure you are familiar with the phrases "gut reaction" and "gut instinct". The solar plexus is instantly reactive in any given situation – it is aligned with the subconscious mind and will react before your conscious mind has time to think.

Interestingly enough, the subconscious mind is like a computer. It can register up to 10,000 messages a day. Because it takes in data verbatim, it does not differentiate between correct and incorrect information – everything is undisputed fact. From the time of your conception and throughout your life, everything that is said, seen, heard and perceived by your senses has been registered. ... The subconscious mind understands only the images that are reflected in the mind ... The subconscious mind does not understand positive or negative WORDS, only IMAGES.

When you imagine what you don't want, the image in your mind is of exactly that but without the 'don't'."

That's how advertising works, they put so many messages out there and we are hypnotised to buy! It makes sense, why don't we teach this at school?? Society would be very different! Maybe there would be fewer braindead morons like my colleagues ... perhaps!

"Interestingly 'Continuously entertaining fears or surrounding yourself with negative people and situations will cause your subconscious mind to know only negativity – and that's what will continue to manifest in your life."

According to Lise, *we should use visualisation to create our ideal life.* That's not a problem, I am a professional daydreamer, I dream about Chris a gazillion times in a day! I know what you are thinking - because I thought it too – if you visualise Chris so much, why aren't you together? Lise says that *"the subconscious mind only reacts to its most recent information. Human beings are continuously inconsistent in their thinking. We must learn to increase our capacity for concentration to focus in order to get where we are going. ONCE YOUR SUBCONSCIOUS MIND SEES THAT YOUR DIRECTION IS CLEAR, YOU WILL GET TO YOUR DESIRED DESTINATION MUCH FASTER."*

And this is so me, I dream of Chris and then I see Stephanie and visualise them together! They are always chatting, flirting, touching, it upsets me! Paws off Stephanie, isn't she happy with one gorgeous man! So from now on I will concentrate my visualisation, Chris is mine!

"START NOW! Visualise your ideal life. Would you like to be surrounded by love?.. to have better relationships with your family? ... to have a job that you find fulfilling? Your subconscious mind will help you achieve everything you desire. It is up to you to learn to work with it and to learn to harness the power that it has. ... Put your subconscious at work on manifesting your perfect job by understanding what that job 'feels' like."

So if I understand correctly Mac, in order to manifest, I must take action, visualise, be specific and feel it. Right, it does not seem to be a difficult task ... or is it?

"Alongside the Subconscious and Conscious Mind we also have a Superconscious Mind. *The SUPERCONSCIOUS MIND is also known as your "Divine Self" or your "GOD SELF". It has a handle on the big picture – your past and future lives, your life plan and which road you need to follow in order to achieve divine perfection. So, when you ask, desire or think you have a real need, make a request to your subconscious mind, but the sure to ask your superconscious mind to let you know if what you want is really beneficial to you. If it is not, you will receive a signal to let go – it will also lead you to a more desirable outcome.... Usually, within a month of your making the request to your superconscious mind, you will experience something radical that will give you a very clear indication as to whether or not your desire was appropriately beneficial – and an alternate will present itself to you.*

How reassuring to know that this power is within you and it is directly connected to the great Universal Power, to the entire cosmos and to the superconscious mind of every human being! Everything is connected – all energy is one!"

I actually don't feel reassured at all! I am not sure I fully get it, there are ways of manifesting all that we want. But if it does not happen it is because it is not good for us? It sounds like a cop out to me? How do I know that it is because I did not do the manifestation work properly? This is beginning to confuse me . . .

"YOUR SUPERCONSCIOUS MIND IS YOUR BEST FRIEND! It is always there to guide and support you, every hour, every minute of your life. Learn to communicate with it, build a relationship with it, and it will never let you down. ... By building this deeply personal and private relationship with your superconscious mind, you will find that you are never along anymore. You can completely trust in its knowledge and know that it has no ulterior motive – only your best interests at heart – because you are one. It will communicate with you through your intuition and advise you in every decision.

You have been receiving signals, or messages, from your superconscious mind since birth, but have not understood their origin. When you are not living in proper alignment with your whole Self, or when you are in a situation that is not beneficial to your spiritual growth, you will experience any number of the following: emotions begin to rule, discomfort and disease (dis-ease) are manifested, you may experience a lack of energy, weight problems, accidents, addiction to alcohol, drugs (prescription or otherwise), your sleep patterns may become disturbed (too much, not enough, or interrupted sleep), your appetite may become erratic, etc."

So if my body looks the way it does is because I am not in alignment with myself... I don't quite understand what this actually means... but as Lise says, I have to start looking inside myself. Again, how do I do that? Hopefully the answers will come in the following pages of this book! Who knows, maybe by the time I finish this book I will have also conquered my weight problems! Forget about dieting; eat all you want, just read 'Listen to Your Body'!!!

I wonder if my superconscious mind thinks that Chris is so good for me? Oh dear, I am obsessed, how many times have I written Chris in this diary? I think if you gave me a penny for each time, I would be a millionaire by now!

So my Superconscious is my best friend. I would like to think that you are my Superconscious as I can tell you everything and know that you will not judge me and I can be 100% authentic with you! Lise suggests that I name my Superconscious mind, so I go for Mac! She suggests "ROUMA", which is amour spelt backwards. But I don't like it, Mac…

Since the day I was born - well not quite, sometimes I can be a tad dramatic - I have always wanted to be skinny. I fluctuate between size 12 and 14, when really I want to be an 8. I think I am quite a healthy eater, I am vegetarian and a lot of celebrities are vegetarian these days and have you seen their bodies? They are super slim and I am not! So what Lise says must have a little truth in it? For sure I am an emotional eater and I drink far too much alcohol, but it is sooo much fun! Me with no Pinot Grigio equals boring Kate!

I eat when I am depressed (which is 79.9 % of the time) therefore I am fat! Lise you are a genius (I am being sarcastic)! And I guess I also drink too much alcohol to mask the pain… of -let's face it -being single. I know that Jamie, Millie and my parents love me, but I do feel terribly lonely and unloved! I think I am a good person, I always aim to please others, I always put others first, love looking after others, I am good at my job (despite my intense dislike for it!), I am not the World's cleverest, but I make up for it with my sense of humour. My face is half-decent, pretty (ish), but yes I am fat but there are lots of fat women out there with boyfriends! Men are such weird creatures! Even super models are cheated on, look at Liz Hurley and Hugh Grant!

I never had much luck with boys. Maybe I give off the bad vibes?? Yes, I will admit it, I don't really follow "the rules". I get drunk, pick up some random guy – although I am not sure I actually do the picking? - sleep with him and then don't hear from him again. I know I should not sleep with guys on the first date if I want a boyfriend. I read in a magazine that men prefer to chase and I don't really give them much of an opportunity! I will put it to the test tomorrow; we are going out to one of my favourite bars, the Drunken Monkey. I need to plan what to wear and will not eat all day tomorrow so I can look fabulous in my faux leather mini skirt! Millie will be out too and she generally gets all the attention from men, but Marco is joining us so...good for me! Jamie is coming too, he always hangs out with me and I think that maybe he deters boys from approaching me. But I love spending time with Jamie, he is so sweet and we make each other laugh. We get each other. There is just no chemistry between the two of us, my Mum thinks it is such a shame. She loves him. But I like fit boys with a dark edge! He is not what one would call a 'bad' boy! I am just like most women, I love a bad boy. That's also maybe why I am still single! Look what happened with Andy last winter. We went out for a month and then he dumped me by text. I mean, that's bad form! Oh what about Nick? We saw each other for 2 months one day he's there, then the next 'puff', he disappears. I never heard from him ever again. Maybe he died!? Or maybe I am like David Blaine and I make people disappear!?

Come back to Earth Kate! I have to keep reminding myself! Let's get back to the task in hand! - Chapter 2 Exercises:

>>*Take a sheet of paper and write down everything you can think of that you now know has been the result of listening to the messages from your subconscious mind. Try to remember as many experiences as you can, pleasant and unpleasant. Perhaps you were afraid something was going to happen and it did. Perhaps you were wishing for something and were surprised when you got it. Without realising it, you were programming your subconscious mind. As you recall each incident and become conscious of how you made it happen, write it down. You will begin to understand that you have always had the power to design your own life.*

When I am at work, I approach my pc with much dread. When I see my boss' name in the inbox, my stomach closes in knots. I know it will be an unpleasant message, and it pretty much is the case! Hate it, hate him!

Every time he (my boss) asks for a meeting, I know that he will have something to say about me, about my work. I don't understand why I have this job if he dislikes me so much?

As for nice incidents . . . well I dream of Chris all the time and he does in fact appear everywhere... but then again the office is not big and we work together!

Nice things don't happen in my life, so I can't really report much else. Come to think of it, I am a master of Food Manifestation! Every time I think of how much I fancy a pizza, we end up having pizza takeaway in the evening. Same thing happens with ice-ream! Maybe I can really start visualising more than just food!

>>*Visualise something specific that you would like to see happen in your life in the near future - over the next few days, perhaps. Keep it simple, but make sure it is of some significance to you and then ask that it happen very soon. Over the next few days, think often about it - feel that you have actually attained it. Believe that you are touching it or experiencing it so that you know, first hand how it feels. Make it seem as real as you possibly can and know deep in your heart that it is coming soon.*

I sooo would like to be with Chris, but if I have to keep it simple... keep it simple, keep it simple??? Oh I know, I saw this amazing electric lime green top in Grazia magazine today. I want to see it in a shop tomorrow, I want to buy it so I can wear it with my lovely faux leather mini skirt. The perfect outfit for tomorrow night will be the electric lime green top, mini skirt and tailored black jacket and knee high boots... not only do I see it, I feel it too... I FEEL great in this outfit!

>>*REMEMBER that the subconscious mind understands neither the past nor the future. It only understands the pictures in the HERE AND NOW. So that, when you are doing the second exercise, tell yourself "I am ", or "I have". You must be able to clearly see yourself with your result and feel your happiness inside.*

>>*It is important that you keep this exercise to yourself, as to share with others will dilute the possibility of success. Unconsciously, you could be influenced by their doubts and opinions and your subconscious mind will pick it up. Focus clearly on the task at hand.*

>>*Repeat the following affirmations whenever you are alone with your thoughts. You will find that you have finally met your closest friend.*

I NOW CONSIDER MY BODY TO BE MY BEST FRIEND AND GUIDE ON EARTH AND I AM RE-LEARNING TO RESPECT, ACCEPT AND LOVE IT AS IT WAS INTENDED.

Boy! I Hope I am gonna slim down to size 8!

Correction! I am slimming down to a size 8

I NOW CONSIDER MY BODY TO BE MY BEST FRIEND AND GUIDE ON EARTH AND I AM RE-LEARNING TO RESPECT, ACCEPT AND LOVE IT AS IT WAS INTENDED –

Get rid of that cellulite Kate!

Good night Mac! I am keeping an open mind and I can't wait to find that top tomorrow!

K x

Friday 8ᵗʰ May 6.30pm

Dear Mac

As 'The Only Way is Essex' lot say, OMG! You will not believe it, I have the top, it's right here on the bed! How amaaazing is that?... Lise's magic is working... Today, at about 12.30pm I went out for a quick lunch with Vicky and as we were walking toward Pret I glanced at the shop to my left (Zara) and saw the top!! It's exactly the way I visualised it, silky, lime green... Can this 'magic' work so fast or is it just a coincidence? You know sometimes we see things, don't really pay attention to them, but then start to notice them everywhere once we are aware of them??

Whichever it is, it does not matter to me today, because I am having a great day and today I want to believe in magic. I now know I will have a magical evening too. Millie, Jamie and Marco are heading off in an hour, so I'd better get ready and have a couple of Sambuca shots to get me in an even merrier mood!

I am so glad that I went through the torture of waxing the other day - being half Italian is not so great when it comes to waxing, I have got hairs everywhere! Thanks Mamma! - I have a strong feeling in my gut that tonight will be my lucky night!

Wish me luck! I will report back tomorrow

Love

Kate x

Saturday 9th May 6pm

Mac, you will never believe it ... I can hardly contain my excitement!

I hooked up with Chris!!!

Oh yes I, Katherine Sophie Arnold, did it! I hooked up with Chris! Last night was THE BEST night of my life!!! I'm on Cloud 9! I feel amazing and totally sexed and loved up!!! I have to keep pinching myself to make sure that I am not dreaming! And I just cannot wipe this big, smug smile off my face!

Everything is a little bit of a blur as I was pretty drunk (3 shots of Sambuca on an empty stomach) when we got to the Drunken Monkey! I remember chatting to Jamie whilst Millie and Marco disappeared somewhere… I reckon they were doing coke in the toilet and some more… they are very rock 'n' roll those two, which is quite amusing as she is a corporate lawyer and he is a banker! Or maybe that's exactly why they have this kind of lifestyle, they are forever at work and they must need something to pick them up? This is such a typical London lifestyle, work hard - play hard … I am not sure it is for me anymore, I want something a little more meaningful in my life. Anyhow, who cares about their lifestyle… I had sex with Chris, I had sex with Chris…

So anyway, going back to my magical night, I was talking to Jamie as I feel a hand around my waist, I quickly turned around ready to punch the arsehole, and to my astonishment it was Chris. I am sure that my face lit up like an Asian Xmas tree! In Asia Xmas trees are super bright and colourful! They do lighting very well in Asia!

And…. Back to the point – why do I jump from one thing to another? Attention span of a gold fish, ants in my pants and all that?? Is it because I am a Gemini?

Goodness ….Chris! Chris!

When he came towards us, my whole body stiffened up on the outside but was tingling with excitement on the inside! My heart was pounding so hard it got louder than the very loud background music! Time stood still, my mouth was dry.

'Kate!?Kate? are you ok' Jamie said pulling me out of the trance!

I introduce Chris to Jamie and although they exchanged pleasantries, I notice that Jamie became a little stiff? I decided to take no notice though as it was so unreal, my very own Ryan

Gosling grabbed my waist and kissed me, yes ME Kate Sophie Arnold, Chris kissed me on the cheek and was clearly flirting with me! He told me how he always found me funny and sexy (MOI? Sexy???). What did he say again? "I love your tits; they are so big I want to stick my head between them!". Sure it sounded a little rude, but he was as drunk as me and anyway he said he loves my tits! I admire his honesty! So to that compliment I said "I might just allow you to do that if you don't tell anybody at work!" and giggled like a little girl. I was so drunk and high -on happiness, not drugs- that, somehow we ended up here at my place and had mind-blowing sex! He is so HOT!

So, first thing this morning he woke up with a Morning Glory, and I am not talking about the green vegetable that grows in South East Asia! He said "Morning Beautiful', grabbed my boobs and let's just say that he knows what to do with his hands, tongue and all the rest!

After medal-winning, Earth-moving performance I made him breakfast: scrambled eggs on toast and black coffee. I did not ask him how he takes his coffee as I already knew. One day at work, I walked into the kitchen, where he was chatting with French bread stick Stephanie. He was making coffee and I took notice of it -the makings of great wife, me! -. As I was making him breakfast it dawned on me that we are work colleagues and have fallen in love and we will be a classic example of an office romance.

After breakfast, more like brunch . . . he took a shower, got dressed in front of me, oh my, he is so confident! How can he not be? All those hours spent at CrossFit, the gym and whatever else are definitely working!!! He gave me a kiss on the lips and left. He is sooo HOT. David Gandy get off my screen saver! I have a picture of Chris to replace you now! Oh I am sooo in love!!

The book is seriously working its magic! Thank you Lise. Now I wonder when he will call or text or e-mail or Facebook message me . . . Positive thinking and all that Kate!

Good night Mac, I am going to run myself a hot bath to calm down. I am now a bundle of happiness mixed with anxiety!

Kate x

Sunday 10ᵗʰ May 10 pm

Evening Mac!

I think I must have checked my iPhone thousands of time, in fact I have lost count. No news from Chris . . . but I think he is playing that silly game, I will wait for 3 days before I call her kind of thing! But then again, I will see him tomorrow at work! Maybe a bunch of fabulous red roses and a thank you card will be waiting for me on my desk? I am such a romantic!

I am still super happy, but I cannot deny that I am feeling a little anxious about the fact that he has not yet got in touch and that I will be seeing him tomorrow. I must find the perfect outfit for tomorrow, for sure a push up bra, he will like that :) (it will accentuate my "great tits"). And I will make sure I take some of those Kalms tablets tonight and tomorrow morning. I hate feeling this way. There are times, especially around that time of the month, when I go through a whole bottle of Kalms. But they do help me loads, I have a bottle here and one at work. When you work with a mental boss like mine you have to take something! I swear he is the reason why I am so anxious all the time!

On a more positive note, Millie seemed to be excited for me, she thinks Chris is hot and she is happy that I finally got laid! On the other hand, Jamie was awfully quiet today, he made little to no eye contact with me. That's really strange. Maybe he felt too hungover and did not fancy talking? He did look worse for wear this morning!

Anyway, my dear Mac, I will now hit my magic book... I am really beginning to think that my Mum is right, this weekend is a very memorable one!

Still no text, e-mail, FB message ...??? Stay calm and positive Kate!

K x

Monday 11th May 8.30 pm

Dear Mac

The magic has left this house. I am so depressed... what a crap, crappety, carp day I had. No Chris... he called in sick!

I was looking rather hot this morning, if I may say so myself. I think I must have lost a couple of pounds over the weekend, that's what love does to me. I remember when I first went out with my Ex Nick, the public school boy, he made me so nervous. I stopped eating for days, oh it was magnificent to feel so light, but at the end of our relationship, Nick did leave me even emptier. He was not so good for my self-esteem. Everything was on his own terms and I convinced myself that I had to change myself and become cool. Nick is a DJ and I thought that he was sooo cool (I still do), but there were always so many girls buzzing around and I was feeling so jealous. My anxiety literally hit the roof! He would say to me "Take a chill pill baby" and I suppressed my feelings by taking the chill pill, namely a handful of Kalms in one go!

It was a very poisonous relationship, he dumped me because he heard some rumours that I went out clubbing and kissed some random guy. I never did that. It was a friend of mine who kissed a random guy – random and Ugleee!! Truth be told, I actually ended up cheating on him whilst he was on a skiing trip! He went away for a week and never once sent me a text. I thought he was cheating so I did too! Insecurity can be a bitch!

Come to think about it, I have seriously poor taste in men! All the boys I end up with always make me feel insecure, I never feel great about myself, shouldn't love feel the opposite? I don't even know if I have ever truly been in love . . . mmmm

Actually you know what Mac, I must stop talking like this, I sound like a stupid victim. Lise says that we need to take responsibility for our actions and emotions. Nick did not make me feel empty, I did. My exes did not make me feel insecure and unloved, I did. At least this is what I think "taking responsibility" means. Last night I read Chapter 3 ' Responsibility and Commitment':

Although, this chapter seems to be very relevant for a parent – hell no! I am never going to be a parent!- there are some bits, that have made me think and appreciate some important things. Here is what Lise explains:

"*RESPONISBILITY is defined a "a moral obligation to assume the consequences of our choices". EACH OF US IS FUNDAMENTALLY RESPONSIBLE FOR HIS/HER OWN EVOLUTION: thereby each of us is responsible for the outcome of our own "soul purpose". Thus, only we are accountable for our own decisions and must accept the consequences of our actions and reactions. "Human Responsibility" does not mean that we are being held accountable for the decisions of others.*

It is a difficult notion to accept, but you have been responsible for your life since before you were born! You chose your parents, your family life and even the country in which you were born. As long as you have the slightest doubt about this, you will not be in a position to change your life. You must understand this concept and take full responsibility in order to become empowered enough to take control of your life"

But what about those poor children who are born in Africa? Do they really choose to be born in such conditions? What about those children who are born in abusive families? I am not sure I get what Lise is saying, although I do agree with the part of taking responsibility for the consequences of my decisions.

"If you are unhappy with the consequences of your decisions, change your decisions. ONLY YOU CAN CREATE YOUR LIFE! In understanding this fully, you will also understand that others are also solely responsible for theirs. Let them take responsibility for their own sake and yours."

I must say, I am quite clear on minding my own business, I don't really interfere in my friends' business, although I am always there to support and listen to them when they need me to. I am a people-pleaser and I will always agree with them as it is important to me that they feel understood.

Millie on the other hand, she is quite bossy and she gets rattled when others don't follow her advice. She really ought to read this chapter. I think that once she has children she will end up being a controlling mother... but as Lise says, it is not my responsibility!

Jamie is more like me, he is such a great listener, not much of a talker! And so wise; mum once told him he is an old soul, is that a compliment?

"Great universal laws have been eternally in place to manage the Universe: they are the physical, cosmic, psychic and spiritual laws that will be maintained regardless of how we choose to behave. We will suffer the consequences of contradicting these laws by experiencing disease, accidents and unhappiness. Breaking physical laws results in very obvious consequences. For example, a person drinking a glass of poison because "it looks like water, so it can't be bad", finds out that his body will react violently. He has broken a physical law. Believing or not in a particular truth does not alter the truth.

The Law of Responsibility is part of the Law of Love, touching the depths of the soul. We are each responsible for ourselves – our "being", our "belongings". Feeling responsible for the actions and feelings of others can result in our own feelings of guilt. This is very uncomfortable for us, even more so when the expectations we have toward others are unmet. Disappointment, anger and frustration are the result – all of which causes despair and disease...

You are not responsible for the happiness of the people around you, whether they are friends, family or co-workers. WHAT YOU ARE RESPONSBILE FOR IS THE WAY YOU REACT TOWARDS THE ATTITUDE PEOPLE HAVE TOWARDS YOU. It is said that "you do not judge the worth of a man by what others say about him, but what he says about others". When others are gentle or violent, critical or loving toward you, it is because you made it happen. Others are your mirror. The way they react toward you is based on the way you react towards yourself unconsciously. You must learn from this.'

OK, now, this is something to digest and absorb... the way my boss treats me is MY responsibility??? He is my mirror??You are wondering the same right? Lise has an answer for that. *"For example: If a certain person is very disagreeable and critical around you and you judge him as disagreeable and a critical person, it is because you are disagreeable and critical with yourself and this person, being a mirror, is only there to help you become conscious of this. If you accept the fact that you are this way, I mean really accept, you will not be bothered by or attract disagreeable or critical people anymore.*

A change in your own attitude will give you the impressions that others around you are changing. The fact is, there is good in everyone - it is up to you to see it. Your thinking is all you have control of – you cannot control others, but your perception of them will change.

You are beginning to understand the notion of personal RESPONSIBILITY! That is why it is so important to become conscious of who you are inwardly – so that you can change your perception and, ultimately your reality."

Got it Mac? Thus the way I judge my boss is my perception based on how I judge myself. He is my mirror! I have to change that perception to start seeing a different person and get on with him. I will give it a go. How lovely would it be to get on with my boss? What about French stick Stephanie? She is so beautiful, is she my mirror? How can it be? We are not in the same league!?? Chris is though!!!

And speaking of Chris, still no sign of the gorgeous demi-god, it is really upsetting me, I wonder if I should send him a message? But I am afraid I will appear to be needy! I can follow the "rules" too! Let him call you, but then again, I have already broken the capital one, don't sleep with him on the first date! I am screwed! Am I? Hope not! Story of my life: no luck with men!

Right Kate, stop thinking about men, let's continue with Chapter 3, which also tackles COMMITMENT. A big, scary word for me!

"COMMITMENT is defined as a pledge of one's Self to a position or a course of action. Commitments can be verbal or written, as in a contract, which binds you to another, whether it be an employee, a spouse, a partner, etc… When one makes a commitment at home, at work or otherwise, even by agreeing to meet someone at a certain time for an appointment or whatever, it is important on a "soul level" to keep the commitment. "YOU REAP WHAT YOU SOW" is one of the greatest laws of life – your integrity and your word are vital to your overall being. You cannot disengage yourself from responsibility, but you can disengage yourself from a previous commitment. Before doing so, be sure to evaluate the consequences, as it can be the precursor to problems in relationships. Before making such decisions, always ask yourself "What will this cost me in regard to my relationship, health, happiness, love…?" Remember – you always reap what you sow."

Got the message loud and clear Lise!!!

"Interestingly, the same applies in your relationship with yourself. If, for example, you've promised yourself that you will exercise every morning. You have made a commitment to yourself. You adhere strictly to your exercise routine for the first few days, but gradually you begin to neglect your commitment. You can't find the time …you forget …finally

the inevitable happens; you have completely stopped exercising. Instead of feeling guilty or becoming critical of yourself, treat yourself as you would a dear friend. Remind yourself that there is no need to be so hard on yourself – accept that you may not have been quite ready to make that commitment for whatever reason and to try again to do so when you feel more prepared. Remind yourself that you have a responsibility to yourself and to those you love to be the best you can be – that you owe it to yourself and to them to be healthy."

I wonder if Lise and I have ever met. When she writes stuff it seems like knows me. What she just described is me! I have joined the gym several times and after a few sessions ended up not going. I have joined running clubs, paid the membership and then never actually went. I have both a monthly membership for hot yoga and only went a couple of times… I am not great at committing to exercise, I've wasted loads on money and feel shit about myself for not doing any exercise! What a catch 22 this is! But Lise might have a point, maybe I am not ready, maybe my motivations are not strong enough? I keep saying that I want to lose weight, I have been saying it for years, but nothing has shifted, not a pound!

Let's see if the exercises can help shed more light on my lack of responsibility and commitment:

>>*Choose a current situation in which you feel someone else is responsible for what is happening to you. Determine your own responsibility regarding the situation, and write it down. What commitments have you made regarding your responsibilities?*

Now get in touch with that person and go over, in detail, what is expected of each of you until it is clear to you and to the other.

In my current state of mind, I can only think Chris. He has not yet got in touch with me. I take responsibility for how I am feeling, but I have not made any commitments. Maybe I can send him a text and see how he is? Commit to do it and feel good about it. At this stage I cannot ask Chris to meet my expectations. Maybe in the future…

All right …. I will text him …

Done, I have set him a text "Hi Chris, hope you are feeling better and look forward to seeing you back at work soon"

I would say, "nice but detached" I don't think I came across as an anxious wreck!

Will he reply?? Breathe Kate, I now choose to be positive, I am peace, I am calm.

>>*Is there a current situation in which you feel responsible for someone else? Accept that that person is ultimately responsible for their own life, their choices and their decisions. Now, contact this person to discuss the issue of personal commitment until clear commitments have been determined.*

These exercises are giving me a headache… I cannot think of anyone in particular. At work people hold me responsible if they are promoted or fired, if they get a pay raise or not. They think that because I am the HR manager I call the shots, but I don't! Their productivity, work performance are their responsibility. I advise my boss, but ultimately he makes a decision on salaries, promotions and bonuses… but then again, I could probably pull a few strings for the right person… Chris perhaps!

>> *Take a sheet of paper and list all the promises and commitments you can think of that you have made to yourself and to others. Which ones have you kept? Are there some from which you can comfortably disengage yourself? From this exercise, you will realise that there are many instances in which you have made commitments that you cannot possibly keep or that you would really prefer not to keep.*

Must we go there? Here are my commitments:

- I will eat healthily
- I will drink less alcohol
- I will exercise more; I will go for a run before or after work every day!
- I will look after myself
- I will lose weight
- I will call my Mum at least once a week
- I will save money
- I will look for another job
- I will meditate every day
- I will say no when I don't want to do something
- I will finish what I start

The list goes on... frankly I don't know why I don't keep my commitments??

Lack of willpower perhaps? Seriously, what is wrong with me? Millie achieves all her goals she sets for herself. Not BUTs, no Ifs!

>> *Write down what you need or want to commit to at this point in your life, both for yourself or for others. Be fair to them and to yourself and be conscious of whether you are overextending yourself. Be conscious, also, of your intent in each situation, remembering that you are not*

responsible for the happiness of others. Again, contact each of the people involved and make the responsibilities of each of these commitments clear to them and to yourself.

Ok the headache is officially turning into a migraine. I am going to leave this exercise; I will do it another time. It takes too much effort and I am also feeling quite depressed at the moment! Still no text from Chris...

>>*Repeat the following affirmation every moment you can, until you understand it fully. Then go onto the next chapter*

I AM THE ONLY PERSON RESPONSIBLE FOR MY LIFE AND I ALLOW EVERYONE AROUND ME TO BE RESPONSIBLE FOR THEIRS.

Got it Lise, from now on, I will own my own shit!

Why as he not text me back yet?! Maybe he is asleep? Maybe he is still unwell? Maybe his phone has run out of battery? Aww ....I will take a couple of pain killers and watch some TV. The fit vampires are on tonight; they will cheer me up!

Good night Mac

K x

PART 2

The Ape is in Love

Dear Mac

The vampires (I am talking about the tv series 'True Blood'!) cheered me up last night and I feel so much better today! Chris was not in the office AGAIN! But he text me! Giant smile!

Text said "Hi Kate, thank you for the message. Sorry I have not been in touch, problems with phone. Had a great time with you and look forward to seeing you again. Chris x"

My heart is still pounding hard, 'x', what a sweet message! He likes me, he likes me… ! And…. my weight loss continues… yesterday I only had a soup and some oat cakes and today I had a couple of apples and some nuts. Millie is cooking dinner tonight for Marco, Jamie and I. She is a great cook – is there anything she can't do? - and I know I am in for a treat :)

I am in such a great mood today, I feel the love! And speaking of Love, here is an account of Chapter 4 of the book, entitled 'Love and Possession'. I am so glad I am still reading this book, although I slacked off yesterday and didn't really do the exercises at the end of the chapter! Bad girl! Smirking whilst writing, I distinctively remember Chris calling me bad girl when he first kissed me!

Chapter 4 Kate, Chapter 4!

What is Love? Love, according to Lise is *"Giving someone all the space and freedom they need. It is also respecting our own needs for space and freedom. Love is respecting and accepting what other people wish to accomplish in their lives. Love is learning to respect and accept others' opinions even though we may not agree with or understand them. Love is giving and guiding without any expectations"*

Mmm, I always thought of love as an amazing connection between 2 individuals (woman and man, woman and woman, man and man) you know just like those films 'The Notebook', 'Love story', 'True Romance'. And love is also what parents feel toward their kids, or what a human being feels towards their pets. I thought that there are so many forms of love, mmm - I am confused.com!!

"Make it your life's goal RIGHT NOW to learn to love with your whole heart. Most people understand the kind of love that comes from the mind: the one that gives you permission to run other people's lives, the one that makes you want to change people and tell them what to do. Even though your intentions may be good and you are convinced your "assistance" is in their best interests, what you are exhibiting in not love, it is POSSESSIVE LOVE. What goes on in other people's lives are their business, not yours. Free yourself to love unconditionally and others will respond in the same way.

We continuously judge and analyse the behaviour of others because we have expectations from them. Again, love is giving and guiding without any expectations. Learn to love in this way."

I must admit, it is still quite a hard concept to get my head around. I completely get it on a level but on the other hand . . . isn't analysing and judging just something that human beings do? Is it not part of life? And would gossip be part of judging? I suppose so? Oh I can't imagine life without gossip, what would I talk about with my friends? Most of our conversations are based around bitching about others! It's fun!

And what about other people judging me? I know for a fact that people judge me completely at work, being HR manager, I am the most hated person by my colleagues and my boss . . . let's not go there. Not nice. But somebody loves me now. It's Chris... Giant smile across my face again!

Oh Chris, every time I think of him I get a warm, fuzzy feeling inside and more ;) Baaad Kate!

Going back to what love really is (according to Lise) ... *"TO LOVE is to accept and respect the other person's wishes, whether or not we understand or agree with them. ... loving entails the respect of other's needs, wants and of their space. Whenever we try to control someone else's words or thoughts, we are not respecting their space. In doing so, you are also losing your own space. With both of your spaces being intermingled in this manner, each of you is suffocating the other. ... In loving someone fully and unconditionally, you may not always agree with that person, but you will accept them without trying to change them. It is the ego that assumes your way of thinking is the correct one. It is the ego that builds expectations."*

Lise goes on about parents and children, but frankly Mac, I am not interested in that part. I don't think I ever will, I am not sure I want a child - too much responsibility! And I will definitely screw them up! But then again, maybe with the right man... For Chris, I might make an exception? He is so gorgeous, and I know I am no Angelina Jolie, but our babies will be so beautiful!

"Most of the problems in relationships between husbands and wives, parents and children – even in the workplace – stem from expectations and poor communication. Because we are not conscious of our actions and thoughts most of the time, our relationships tend to remain on the

level of possession and manipulation. Accept and understand that no one is responsible for anyone else's happiness! When someone wants to please you or you want to please them, it is the icing on the cake! LEARN TO BAKE YOUR OWN CAKE – ENJOY IT ON YOUR OWN! If someone wants to enjoy your cake with you, to share your happiness – THAT'S THE ICING ON THE CAKE!"

I very much enjoy the analogy of baking cakes, baking is my number one hobby! I just feel so relaxed when I bake. It's my meditation, I guess, I have never meditated! I often bake cakes after work to wind down! I also love eating my cakes! They are yummy and I do have a sweet tooth, I take after my dad with that! And that's probably why I am so fat? Well, not so fat now! I have lost at least 5 lbs in 5 days!

From cakes to books, as all respectable Self Help Books, it carries on with the omnipresent YOU HAVE TO LOVE YOURSELF BEFORE YOU LOVE OTHERS! Talk about cliché… Lise's version is: *"Few people really understand what this means. In truly loving yourself or others, the two essentials ingredients are RESPECT AND ACCEPTANCE. Your relationships with others will improve a thousand fold once you have learned to love and respect yourself. Respect your own space and you will be able to respect others. Accept yourself as you are and grow from there and you will learn to accept others as they are.*

Treat yourself firmly but gently – do not judge yourself when you have done something that you think is non-beneficial to you (some would call this a 'mistake'… but it is actually a 'learning experience'). Often this is the only way to become acquainted with a particular 'consequence'. Continue to learn and grow, maintaining your own garden (your inner Self), your own space, and everything around you will begin to exhibit balance and harmony. … Love has tremendous healing power. It is a powerful vibration. When you are filled with love, those vibrations are so strong that people around you will feel better in your presence. You will think that others have changed, but they are only responding to your positive vibrations. Again, they are your mirror.

What does it mean to "LET GO"? How does it happen? It happens when you decide to stop wanting to change others or yourself. It happens when you just accept yourself and others as they are, unconditionally… and when it happens, the transformation begins. You will begin to witness miracles."

I am going to take a break here Mac, Millie is calling, she needs help with setting the table! But I will be back and do my chapter 4 exercises, I shall not get drunk at dinner, this love business is too important to me to skim over it. I want my relationship with Chris to have a happy ending and not the sleazy kind! What is wrong with me and these sexual innuendos ☺ Aww, I got myself so excited, I hardly want to eat. One thing is for sure, Love is the best weight loss antitode!

10.30 pm . . . Hello, hello again Mac

Yum dinner was great! And I only had one glass of wine. I left Millie and Marco finishing the bottle (and knowing them a lot more bottles will follow…) I just hope the sex is not going to be too loud, they are quite noisy! My room is next door to Millie's and well… anyway… Jamie was awfully quiet tonight, he hardly made eye contact with me, was perfectly polite and friendly, but I sense some weird energy. Maybe he is not feeling very well, he hardly touched his food and did not have a drop of alcohol. He told Millie he doing a detox. Good for him, hopefully once the detox kicks in he will brighten up?!

I promised that I would do the exercises . . .

>>*Think of one simple thing that would bring you happiness and do it*

Kiss Chris! But he is not here..sooo, errm, I know...light up my favourite candle, it's a Space NK, Mediterranean Fig, it smells divine and reminds me of when Chris was in my bed! ... ...There it is.. hmmm gorgeous, it puts me in a great, loving mood.

>>*Ask one other person what simple thing would bring them happiness and help them to accomplish it. If it requires an investment of time and/ or money on your part, be sure to discuss your limitations.*

I could ask Mum, but then again I know what she will say ..."what makes me happy is to see my Kate happy!" Well, Mamma Dearest, I am working on it ...Chris is the key to my happiness and this time I will do my best not to screw up this relationship, this time I will be cool and take a hold of my anxieties!

>>*In summary, take the time to consciously bring yourself one piece of happiness at a time and to do the same for someone else.*

I am not sure what Lise means here, but what I am going to do is work on staying positive every day from now on!

>>*Repeat the following affirmation every moment you can until you understand it fully.*

I RESPECT AND ACCEPT THE WISHES AND OPINIONS OF OTHERS WHETHER OR NOT I AGREE WITH OR UNDERSTAND THEIR REASONS. CONSEQUENTLY, I RADIATE AND RECEIVE MORE AND MORE LOVE

Good night Mac . . . I think this Love stuff is sinking in

K x

Dear Mac

I had a great day! Finally, Chris was back in the office! As I walked into the office, I glanced over his desk and there he was! Basking in his glorious light, an angel on earth! He cagily said hi and when I got to my desk the most beautiful e-mail was waiting for me! "Hi Kate, how is it going? Fancy catching up this Saturday? Maybe cinema, drinks and then back to your place?"

I love that he is straight to the point! 'Back to your place', he so fabulous!

I replied "Hi Chris, I am very well, thank you, it's great to see you, I hope you are feeling better. I would love to spend Saturday evening with you!"

Chris: "Cool, we can do the Odeon in Islington, the new James Bond film just came out, would you like to see that?"

Now Mac, I am not big on James Bond movies, being a woman I find them rather patronising, but relationships are all about compromise right? :)

And if there is something that I have learned from the Love Chapter, Love is about accepting others without judging!

My reply: "I'd love to, I adore James Bond movies!" a white lie in the name of love!

His reply: "Excellent! x" Oh kisses . . . kisses . . . I can't wait to be in the arms of my very own Chris Hemsworth, mmmm!

The rest of my day was pretty busy with meetings, which is just as well as my head was spinning, my stomach was in knots, I am in love.

I honestly believe that Lise' s book is really changing my life, it seems to me that since I have started reading it and doing the exercises, magic stuff has been happening in my life and although I still don't fully like my reflection in the mirror, I am starting to like myself more. I am no Jennifer Aniston nor Angelina Jolie, but a demi-God like Chris wants me! There must be something about me after all! How can this be possible? And this love stuff is definitely making me slimmer, I think I am almost down a dress size and in such short space of time! Lise, maybe you should add to your book that Love is the best weight loss diet!

And just as I thought that things could not get any better, I go and read Chapter 5 'Cause and Effect', true magic, get this…

"Understanding *the immutable Cosmic Law of Cause and Effect will help you become the master of your own destiny. Simply put, action causes reaction or 'you reap what you sow'. What you put into your life is what you will get out of it."* I think this is what they call Karma! *"Cause and Effect is a Universal Law governing the physical, mental, psychic, cosmic and spiritual worlds. Not to "believe in it" is just as senseless as denying the law of gravity… Everything you reap in your life was sown in your conscious and unconscious thoughts. Those are the seeds of your reality, so be aware if what you are planting.* Great example of *this - Right now, do you think it is possible for you to be living in a million dollar house? No? It's not for you – it's only for "rich people", right? There you are! You reap according to your thoughts. Why is it there are so many people living in mansions? There are thousands of millionaires! Why them and not you? Only because THEY BELIEVE IN IT!"*

Emoji explosion bombs...

To me this is quite ground-breaking. I never thought much of my thoughts, I never understood that thoughts and beliefs affect everything in life, what I put out in any sort of form (thoughts, words, actions) I get back ....

For example, I always say that I don't have enough money. It appears that this belief and thought that keeps me poor! I can't leave my job 'cos I will not find another one or (and this is my particular favourite), I hate my job, but I don't know what else to do! Nobody loves me (well somebody does now :)), I am fat, I am ugly, I am a loser, shit always happens to me, you get the picture!!!

"If you want to change the effect and the results in any area of your life, you only have to change their causes. Take a look at what you reap and look back to verify what you have sown. Undoubtedly, you will find the cause. ... If you don't understand why some situations keep repeating themselves in your life, remember that what you reap has been sown by you from as far back as childhood. If you decided as a young child to feel sorry for yourself, you will continue to do so into adulthood. This particular programming may manifest itself as poor health, emotional illness or a violent temper. Your probably do not remember making such decisions, because they are usually made unconsciously. However, it is not necessary to go as far back as your early childhood in order to understand the concept. You can start a new chapter of your life RIGHT NOW! You can change the effects you are experiencing by starting this minute to change the causes."

This is amazing news, I need not worry about the Past anymore, need not to analyse everything, all I need is a decision to change things right now! Seems pretty easy, it's so inspiring, so liberating, so freeing . . . I feel really good right now, I feel like my life is full of possibilities!

"The basic steps to getting what you want:

- *Clearly determine what you want and visualise it*
- *Live it in your mind until you can touch it, taste is and deeply feel the join in it*
- *Take action*

REMEMBER: YOU WILL ONLY GET WHAT YOU EXPECT TO RECEIVE! *The rewards may not come instantly, but DON'T GIVE UP! Perseverance is essential."*

FABULOUS!!! FABULOUS! FABULOUS! I am excited to do the exercises. This is fun!

Chapter 5 Exercises

>> *Make a list of the goals you would like to reach by tomorrow. Do the same for the goals you would like to reach over the next week and the next year. The only limitations are those that you will place on yourself.*

Get out of my job, marry Chris, be a size 8, be a millionaire .... all right, all right, I do have a playful sense of humour but no, seriously these are my goals! I am just not sure that I can achieve them by tomorrow, but long term yes! As for tomorrow... mmm... I want to..erm... oh I got it . . . go to the Pilates class I signed up for! I keep signing up but never go. I am such a procrastinator! Pilates is great for toning, especially the bulging pooch, which by the way is definitely going down!

I also would like to stick to my new positive thinking. To have a good day at work without feeling ridiculed by my boss and …needless to say see the love of my life, Chris, of course :) !!!

>>*Over the next three weeks, become more conscious of the negative and unnecessary attitudes that could become obstacles in you achieving these goals. Transform these thoughts into positive ones that will help you get what you want. Take a close look at your attitude!*

I have got to start seeing my job as a blessing … after all, it does pay the bills, my drinking habits, my clothes, my pilates classes – the ones I book and never make! – my shoes …and more … you see! I an be positive!

>>*Repeat the following affirmation as often as you can.*

AS OF NOW I SOW AND I REAP WITH MY THOUGHTS, WORDS AND ACTIONS, ONLY WHAT IS BENEFICIAL TO ME

I got this!! I really feel that I do!

Good night Mac . . . Love the new Positive Kate x

Rosaria La Pietra

Dear Mac

Wow! This positive thinking stuff is harder than I thought! Example, Stephanie! Every time I see her and Chris together, I get these very mean thoughts in my head, they are not positive at all!... "Leave him alone, you stick thin Frenchie, eat some bread for the love of God, you've got your own amaaazing boyfriend, leave my man alone. Your accent is hideous, Bitch! I want to feed you Baguettes and Croissants till you get fat!" Not nice right? But she always flirts with him and today she took it to another level! She made me feel so insecure. She is so pretty, skinny with big boobs, French accent (Men love it, why?), long glossy brown hair and so well put together! Arrrrgh!

Anyway...focus, focus, positive energy, positive energy...Nope, can't do it, it's too far out! She has got into the core of my bones and I cannot shake her!

And what's up with people in London?? They are always in such a hurry, nobody smiles, they bump into you and don't even acknowledge it! Rude, rude, rude!

There! It's all out of my system! GOOD things have ALSO happened today!

I made the Pilates class, it was sooo hard, but I utterly enjoyed it!! No pain no gain they say.

And of course Chris! His smile makes me go weak at the knees (and more!), but I did not like his flirting with Stephanie! Woman get your paws off my man!

He also sent me an e-mail, which tops the one he sent me yesterday! "Good morning Beautiful, you are looking gorgeous today. I can't wait to get my hands all over your hot body!" Oh I am in love, love, love!

I am also making progress with the book. Today I read chapter 6 'The Ties that Bind'. I must admit, I am not sure I got it, perhaps re-writing the main points will help me to capture the meaning more.

'The ties that I refer to are the invisible cords that have been forming since birth – the ones that, because of your reactions, continue to bind you to those who have been authority figures in your life; parents, grandparents, older siblings, relatives, baby –sitters, neighbours, teachers etc. Whatever you refused to accept in them produced a lingering bond that continues to keep you tied to those people and situations.

… The first decision you ever made is this life, although you will not remember, was choosing your parents. In choosing them, you were accepting and loving them as they were. Even so, right from birth, you would surely have liked to change some of their behaviours as it pertained to you. Each attitude not accepted has formed a "cord". The invisible tie, always present between you and your parents, creates an inner irritation. It remains there to remind you that you are exactly like what you did not like in your parents. This is true of everyone you have ever judged.'

I know Mac, WTF? We choose our parents? Although I am not sure about that, I can sort of see what Lise means. My dearest Mum for example! And you know when I say dearest, I am being very sarcastic! I do love my mum, but I just don't get her ways, her way of thinking. The best way to describe her is new age hippy!

Vegan food, holistic medicines, faux leather bags, anti fur (well I am too!), animal activist, she never says anything bad about anyone, she always see the best in everyone, she is a Buddhist! She is so holy; I just think she is fake! Nobody can be so positive all the time.

And she really gets me worked up (I guess these are the inner irritations Lise is talking about) when she says that she was just like me when she was younger! Oh MY God! Arrgh! We are nothing like each other! I am a lot more like my dad. Laid back, generous, quiet and unlike my mum very much in touch with reality. Although I do get my full lips and thick hair from her!

Anyhow, Lise (the mind reader!) replies to my thoughts. *'You have probably put so much effort into being the opposite of your mother, that you are preventing yourself from expressing your own personality. Whether you are exactly the same or determined to be the opposite, you are still reacting and carrying that baggage with you. In trying so desperately to be different from your mother, the cord is even harder to break than if you were the same'.*

Arrgh, headache coming up. Could this be true?? I am not expressing my own personality??I am nothing like my Mum! We really have nothing in common, apart from looking a little alike!

'In order to break this tie with your parents and finally give yourself permission to be who you really are, you must accept your parents

(or other authority figure) did what they could to the best of their knowledge. They loved you the best they knew how and in the only way they knew how. ...

As you continue to hold a grudge, your egos grow. You believe that you've been treated unfairly. You will carry this around with you at an enormous price! This "chip on your shoulder" will be costly in every relationship you become involved in and your health and happiness will be permanently in jeopardy as your body and Superconscious mind persistently send you messages that remind you that you are going against the Universal Law of Love. There is no escape other than FORGIVENESS!'

FORGIVE MY MOTHER?? I don't even know how you do that? And I am not even sure I need to forgive her ...I will have to think it over ... maybe the exercises will help

>> On a sheet of paper, write down everything you can remember that bothered you about your parents during your early childhood (from birth to approximately 18 years old)

>>List the things that bothered you about other people who influenced you during the same period

My parents walking around naked! I absolutely hated it! Put something on please! I used to scream in my head!! I don't want to see bits dangling around! Aww ... and something that I have never told anyone! I heard them have sex several time, it was absolutely disgusting! I mean who wants to hear anyone have sex, let alone see their parents!?? It's effing disgusting!

My Mum was and still is an animal activist and, Miss Save the World! Protect the animals here, protect the women of Africa there, PETA, Amnesty International, WWF, arrgh! - If only mum paid more attention to me and my needs!!!

I know it is very noble of my mum to want to look after all the innocent and defenceless beings (animals and people) of this planet, but I often felt like my needs were never met by her. I would not go as far as saying that she neglected me, but she pretty much left me to me, she always said that she could trust me, ' you are such a lovely, responsible and independent young lady', she used to say and still does! And yes I am, but a I would have liked my mum to spend more time with me, to take me clothes shopping, to be a bit more present!

And my dad?? I don't know... he was playing golf most of the time, I can't say that I spent much time with him. Although the little time I did spend with him, I recall being fun. My dad is a very quiet man, he is quite funny, and pretty much the opposite of my mother. He is not spiritual at all, but they accept each other and in their odd way, they get on and the love each other. I think ... I don't really spend much time with them nor I speak to them that much.

They left London when I was 16 to go live in Ibiza, but I decided to stay behind. Ibiza was not so great back then, London is a much more exciting place for a teenager! Thankfully they agreed to let me live with my grandparent in London.

My grandparents were great. My parents were successful property investment entrepreneur, they did really well financially and they decided that instead of hiring a nanny, they would move my grandparents from Italy into our big house. Very big house in

Blackheath. I love my grandparents, they are Italian and thanks to them I learnt loads! I am fluent in Italian, I love Italian food, I can even cook it! Vegetarian style of course, they were the most generous, kind-hearted and warm. But boy they fed me! Every time they sow me sad, they would give me food. Food when I was sad, food to congratulate me for my achievements, food when I was unwell, food when I was well. That's why I was a very chubby child and teenager! Mind you, I still am now. Well not now that I am in love, now that I have dropped down to almost a size 10. Come to think of it, I may have found a new a successful diet, LOVE! Has somebody already written this kind of diet book?

Despite how wonderful my grandparents have been, I still longed to have a proper relationship with my parents. I just feel they were absent for most of my life. Sure enough they were always in contact over the phone, e-mail, but they were not really there for me, not like my grandparents. And if you are wondering where my grandparents are not, they have gone back to Italy. They just could not hack the weather in London and I don't blame them! I see them at Christmas every year and during summer I often take a week off to visit. They are always so happy to see me and they always feed me with the best food in Italy!

>>*Choose one of the situations listed and go through the process of accepting responsibility for your part in it. Using the same situation, see the love that was underlying. Then, go to them in person and express what you are feeling. Forgive them and ask them for forgiveness.*

This is really hard for me. I don't really like confrontation and I don't have much of a "deep" dialogue with my parents. I remember once whilst on holiday in Ibiza. I got so drunk and got so mad at my mum for no reason whatsoever. Sometimes just her presence is enough to make me mad! But I am never able to actually have an adult conversation with her. Adrenaline raises, I start to cry and so walk away! I am guessing I have a lot of pepped up emotions towards her.

But I feel somewhat different now, now that I am in love, I feel like I can make more an effort. I feel like I can let go of energy thing now. After all what is the use in bringing back the past? What's the point in getting me and her upset?

>>IMPORTANT- *It is essential that this exercise be done before going on to the next chapter. You may find that a lot of emotions will surface. Don't be afraid – you are opening doors that will lead you to your freedom*

>>*Repeat this affirmation as often as possible*

I FORGIVE EVERYONE I JUDGED AND I NOW BREAK FREE FROM THE TIES THAT PREVENT ME FROM BEING IN HARMONY WITH MYSEF. I LOVE MORE AND MORE WITH MY HEART.

>>*If there is someone with whom it is especially difficult to feel love, here is an affirmation that will help you open your heart:*

I FORGIVE (name of person) MUM COMPLETELY, REGARDING (situation or attitude in question) FOR NOT BEING THERE FOR ME IN MY CHILDHOOD AND I WANT ONLY GOODNESS FOR YOU. THEREFORE I FORGIVE MYSELF FOR HAVING THE SAME ATTITUDE, FOR I BECOME WHAT I JUDGE.

I become what I judge? I am nothing like my mother? Once again, I am not sure I get what Lise is wanting to say here, it is such a new concept for me … but I will sleep on it, it might sink in??

Good nice Mac

Love

K x

Friday 15ᵗʰ May

Dear Mac

I have practiced Forgiveness today! I think. (?) This love stuff is amazing…

This morning my boss was his usual grumpy mood, I think his 27 year old wife is proving to be a bit of a handful. Gossip in the office has it that she spends more that he earns!! They have 4 children and 4 nannies! I mean 4! Children! Isn't this world over populated? I don't think I am ever going to have children, I don't know really like them! They are little monster sucking the life out of you! That's maybe why she has a nanny for each child?

Anyway, this is another story. My boss celled me the phone and barked ' Kate, we need to discuss the Finance Officer vacancy' and slams the phone down. No 'please', no 'thank you'. So I march into his office and I sit down, for the first time I see how miserable he actually is and I feel a deep sense of compassion building in me. As I observe this sense of compassion, I notice that I start to relax and I start to appreciate what a brilliant man he actually is. And … to my surprise at the end of the meeting he says, 'Thank you Kate, I appreciate your work'! Hello!!!!??? This is the very first time he has ever thanked me! A miracle! I starting to believe that that magic is happening in my life!

I am beginning to appreciate that everybody comes with their baggage and when they are grumpy, bitchy (Stephanie!), Saddos (many people in my office), they are just unhappy! I am not perfect, but I would like to think that I am polite (most of the time!), don't bitch much, unless it's deserved (Stephanie!) and these days am learning to be happy! Since the day Lise (through her book) and Chris have come into my life I have been a lot happier! Millie and Jamie are still my best friends, although lately I have not really seen much of them. Millie is spending lots of time with Marco and Jamie is very distant these days, he is hardly ever at home. I wonder what is going on. I send him lots of texts, but he takes ages to reply back and he says he is busy...??? doing what? He does not have a life! Oh well, I am busy too, I am dating the love of my life and I am re-building myself. Today has given me fresh motivation to carry on with the book and the exercises.

Chapter 7 of the 'Listen to Your Body', BTW, My

body is shrinking by the day! Love and Forgiveness are doing wonders for my body! I am shrinking, although that hideous cottage cheese is still plaguing my thighs! Arrgh!.... Forgive cellulite?? NO WAY! GO AWAY!

Chapter 7 is titled 'Faith and Prayer'. And Mac, I know what you might be thinking, what? Faith? and what Prayer?... I am not religious at all! As far as I am concerned religion is dangerous and it is used to control the masses! But actually Lise does not mean it like that. Here it goes Mac, key points of my understanding. And I quote Lise as it is quite tricky to put these concepts down in my own words. Well, you might have noticed that I have been doing it from the start! You might have also noticed that I am not very structured in my thinking and that I jump from one thing to the other, I get easily distracted and I have the attention span of a gold fish. You might be wondering how I manage to keep my job? Easy it's all down to my assistant Vicky! She is so organized, she is awesome! But then again, she is a Virgo and I am a Gemini... ☺ Virgos are very organised people. Geminis are a little more... scatter brain ...like me! Or maybe it's just me?

Where was I .... See what I mean! Maybe Vicky should organize my journaling too! ☺

'The Scriptures (I am not sure what she means, but stay with me) *define faith as "the confirmation of our hopes and the evidence of the unseen". When you are motivated by faith, your trust in a knowledge that is not limited by your own belief system. You know, deep down in your heart, that there is a much bigger picture and you are convinced that you will get what you deserve and desire from the unlimited resources provided by the universe'*

Ok no, I don' t have faith then ... honestly it is something I never really contemplated, it's new territory to me,

'Almost two thousand years have passed since JESUS delivered his message of love and faith to the world. It's time we started living according to his profound and vital teachings. To have faith is to have an unshakable trust in GOD's presence within ourselves. We are taught to pray by saying "GOD help me". In saying this, we are referring to our inner GOD. He does not exists "somewhere out there, governing the

Universe from afar", but within the hearts of every living being. When you see yourself as a living manifestation of GOD and when you feel His great power within you, you can achieve anything you desire, such is the power of Faith'

Far out! (emoji bomb symbol)

Although these concepts are quite hard to digest - partly because my mum, always says to me ' Kate you are enough, you are great, I have faith in you, I always have and always will! I know that you always make the right choice and that you will find peace in your life' (what a saint she is! Holy Mother of Kate!) I guess I have not quite forgiven her yet . . . . I sort of get it.

Look Mac, here I am writing on you, through you, I have access to e-mails, internet, skype, iPhone, TV, I don't even know how it all works, but it does. And every night I switch you on and every night I know that you will not let me down! That's faith too, for sure

On the other hand, to have Faith in me? That's another matter. I am turning 30 next month and my life has been pretty much a total failure. However ...the reason that I am writing this journal, reading this book, doing these exercises is because deep down I know that I owe it to myself to be happy. I deserve to be loved, I deserve to have the career of my dreams – even though I don't yet know what that is, I deserve to make more money, I deserve it all!

Lise says that *'Believing it' before 'seeing it' is faith.* And you know what, I saw Chris and me together, I believed in us before we got together, and although we just started seeing each other, I have faith that we will go very far. I always see us getting married on the beach, wearing white ... on a white sandy beach ...turquoise blue ocean, orchids everywhere … maybe Thailand? Maybe Bali? We look into each other's eyes…. He tells me that he will love me forever … aww … amazing!

And …. there are steps to building faith …

STEP 1: Ask

STEP 2: Believe

STEP 3: Receive

V. interesting paragraph: *'Once you have more faith in yourself, you will discover that you have more faith in others. It's a marvellous discovery! You will no longer be influenced by negative people once you realize **that everything happens inside of you**, rather that outside of you, and those of faith will be drawn to each other.*

When I read that everything happens inside of me, I feel my brain exploding in my skull! It's a very strong concept. How can it be? Have I been making myself miserable all these years? Have I caused myself all this pain? I thought that things just happen and that bad things always happen to good people! Millie, Jamie and I we always talk about how unlucky we are! Have we really made all of this stuff up?

Maybe the exercises will help me grasp this concept a little more …

-   **TAKE A LEAP OF FAITH. Choose something you have wanted for some time and decide RIGHT NOW to make it happen.**

Mmmmm, oh I know! For a while I having been toying with the 'Cake Baking' course. I absolutely love cakes! Yes I know, you can tell by looking at my size of my behind! But seriously, every time I walk past patisseries, I am always in owe of how beautiful their cakes look! I know I am good baker, but I have learnt from google. I really would love doing a course and learn properly. Let's do a search and see what comes up ...

Found one! Let's take the bull by the horns (and I am not talking about those poor bulls in Spain and Argentina! My mother is working with PETA to abolish bull fighting! Horrible stuff the corridas!) I will book the course! It's Millie's Birthday soon, I can surprise with a beautifully designed and lusciously tasting chocolate cake!!!

- **If you need to put a deposit down on something material, on a vacation package, whatever - do it, If starting the ball rolling entails making a phone call to someone, do.**

The course is booked!

- **DO IT WITHOUT FURTHER DEALY! in Life, "being" should always precede "having". If you are thinking 'When I win a large amount of money in the lottery, I will buy the house of my dreams and then I will be happy', you are going against the natural laws.**

I am professional pastry chef!

- **Don't wait until (fill in the blank) .... I MARRY CHRIS!! to be happy. Be happy first, take action. You will have what you desire.**

- **Repeat the following affirmation and go to the next chapter**

I BELIEVE IN THE GREAT DIVINE HERITAGE WITHIN ME AND I DRAW FROM IT, EVERYTHING I NEED WHENEVER I NEED IT.

Hang on Mac, I just got a text . . .

OMG, It was Chris, ' can't wait to get my hands on your tits tomorrow night!' sweet, so sweet!... perhaps a little rude? maybe he is tipsy, it is Friday night after all . . . and I am thinking of baking cakes and marriage, rock on Kate! . . . but tonight I did not fancy going out at all .... I want to be rested and in super form for my date with Chris tomorrow.

I am planning to go for a run in the morning, followed by Pilates. And then I will spend the whole afternoon beautifying, gotta shave my gorilla legs and find the perfect outfit!

Mac, I going to watch a film now, what an amazing day! The text from Chris is the icing on the cake! The Love cake, a dark chocolate heart shaped cake with a huge amount of icing on top!

Love and Peace

Kate x

Before my date with Chris

Dear Mac

I am so excited about date night with Chris! Millie is not around, her phone is switched off and Jamie left the house at 7.30 this morning, I never get to see him or chat to him these days!

Anyway, I have been a very good girl so far today! Naughty girl will come out a little bit later, if you know what I mean ;)

I went for my jog, jogged all the way to South Bank and back and did my Pilates class at 11. I expect I will be very sore tomorrow and in many places :). I am sorry, my mind keeps wandering to ... well, let's face it, SEX!

But let's get serious now, what should I wear? well, well, naturally something that shows my cleavage, Chris is so fond of it, and maybe, yes why not, legs too! I am practically a size 10, a little tight, but Kate thinks positive, I am a 10 :)

Perfect! I have this wonderful little black number in my closet. I bought it from Mango a couple of years ago, it's a size 10 and never actually worn it as I could never fit in. Whey do us women buy clothes that we know don't fit?? Is it because are romantic dreamers, we hope that one day we will be able to wear a fab dress to the best date of our life? Let's how it fits, hold on Mac.

It fits, it fits, it fits . . . I look amazing in it, if I can say so myself! It hugs my curves perfectly, perhaps a little tight around the chest area, I struggle to breath, by boobs are pushed all the way up to my throat!

LBD (aka little black dress), denim jacket and black wedges. Fierce, if I may say so myself! Naturally I also need to shave my legs, cos body my hair grows so quickly, it's crazy! Maybe I can collect all the hair that I shave and wax and sell it to people that make Gorilla fancy dress costumes! There goes a business niche! Ha! You see there is positive in everything!

So good bye for now Mac, wish me good look for tonight, I feel it will the best date of my life so far!

Kate x

Sunday 17th May,

Date: James Bond movie, drinks, sex

Aww Mac! If I thought I was in love with Chris, now I know, **I am in love with Chris! Kate <3 Chris**

It's not lust, we are so compatible, have similar taste, we have amazing chemistry.

Here is an account of how it went last night

We met at the Odeon cinema in Islington, he was wearing a super sexy black leather jacket, black t-shirt, blue jeans and brown Palladium shoes. I basically melted as he looked at me with those amazing deep blue eyes . . . he told me I looked sexy and he kissed me on the lips. As a true gentleman he had bought my cinema ticket, sweet popcorn (although I am more of a savoury popcorn kinda gal!) and one giant diet coke. I said thank you, but I did not touch the stuff! I don't want him to think that I eat at any opportunity I get. I want him to think of me as refined and sophisticated. I figure popcorn is not the most refined nor sophisticated! I do love cinema popcorn though! The smell brings great memories of when I was a teenager and the great films Millie, Jamie and I used to watch. We used to get a large box of popcorn each!

But I am almost 30 now and I am going out with the most amazing man in the whole of London and he just happens to like me. I can give up the popcorn. And it was a good move on my part as Chris told me hates people who munch on popcorn during movies! Phew!

I did however share his drink, my mouth kept going dry every time he held my hand during the film. I mean, it all got too hot for me … I needed a drink I wish there had been rum in it though. I could not relax a bit!

As you can imagine, my mind was not on the film at all, I was sooo nervous, excited and … "excited" to be sitting next him! He smelt divine, masculine and fresh! Sitting next to him was electrifying, there was nooo way that I could concentrate on the film, which is just as well, James Bond movies are not for me. I find them incredibly sexist. But we are all different and Chris enjoyed it a lot, he even said that I could be a Bond girl, apparently I got what it takes? What no brain?

After the film, we went for a drink. The pub was packed, but as we entered the room, it was as though the world had stopped, everybody looked at us, I might be paranoid but I think I overheard somebody say " what is he doing with her? He should be with me".

Jealous cow! He is mine! But he does make me feel so anxious and on edge. I just had to get drunk! Chris is tall, I would say 6 feet tall, broad muscle bound shoulders, fit as hell, amazing set of teeth and thick hair. Beautiful nose ... just perfection!! and did I mention that he also smells heavenly? Oh yeah I did! Before he started at our company he used to work for Abercrombie & Fitch. He wanted to get into finance as he felt he could do better than showing his abs and flirt with customers. Too right! He is very clever and ambitious too.

Chris was so flirtatious, full of sexual innuendos, and I found it so sexy, I felt really wanted! To know that a God like Chris wants me, makes me feel very special, a Goddess! A large dose of Vino helps too!

The chemistry between us sizzles, I can't even remember how, and what time, we got home. Sadly, and a feel a little embarrassed to admit it, I had a bit too much to drink and I can't quite remember the sex. I know we had a great time, and I want to shout it from the roof tops, I AM IN LOVE WITH CHRIS, I LOVE CHRIS! I wonder how he feels about me? I hope I was not too much of a drunken mess as it is not very sophisticated! What a shame that I don't remember everything, it is a fuzzy love memory! Who cares anyhow?

My love for him is making me re-evaluate myself, I think my true self comes out when I am with him. I feel he has so much faith in me and wants to make me a better person. This morning at breakfast for example, we went to the Luxe Bar for breakfast. He ordered a full English (bless him! He must have used so much energy last night:) and I had my usual Vegetarian version. Chris asked me why I am a vegetarian. I said that I was raised that way, I actually don't know any different. And of course I love animals! Chris made an excellent point though. He said that he loves animals too but it is natural for humans to eat animals. It's nature's law. 'Lions don't worry about killing a zebra when they are hungry!' He suggested I try some bacon. 'Bacon is sick'... he said. So to show him that I am very open minded, I tried it. After all why should I be a vegetarian just because my mum raised me that way? He looked at me pride and added 'Kick this veggie bullshit, meat is good for you! I think he has a point. I have decided to introduce meat and fish into my diet! I won't tell my mum though; she is going to start with a lecture on how human beings exploit animals.

Time has come to get my own identity and cut the ties with Mum! Chris's energy is so strong and contagious, I am changing for the best, for the first time in a very long time I feel happy with myself! A brand new Kate!

And speaking of energy, 'Energy' is the title of chapter 8 of 'Listen to your body'. This chapter to me is very much out there, it talks about Chakras. Chakras What? I have no idea what they are, but the concept of energy is very interesting.

'Do you have enough energy to make the most of your day or would you like to have more? Most of us would give anything for a little more energy! Researchers in California discovered that the human body has, potentially, enough energy to light a city like Montreal or New York for a whole month!

Nothing creates energy like POSITIVE ANTICIPATION! Motivation and satisfaction generate tremendous personal energy that fuels you to realize your goals. This energy will make all the difference in your quality of life!' OK this makes sense to me, that's why I now feel so empowered and in charge! The re-birth of Kate!

'Running out of energy is a signal from your body and your Superconscious mind that you are not living in harmony with yourself. You are cutting yourself off from the source and expending energy without recreating more. You are depleting your energy resources and only what motivates you will replenish them'.

This must be the reason why I feel so tired and exhausted after a long day at work. Yes, I am busy, but I am bored and tired of dealing with office politics, with my colleagues and my boss! But when I arrange to go out for drinks after work, I get a surge of energy. Up until now I always thought it was alcohol, but maybe it's down to the energy force!

'The physical body is surrounded by an invisible and more subtle body. This body is composed of a magnetic energy field that looks like thousands of small lines surrounding the physical body. At seven precise locations in the body, twenty-one of these lines converge to form areas of energy called "Chakras".'

I am not going to go there Mac! I honestly don't get what these chakras are and I don't see how relevant they are to me. Just know that there are 7

1. **Base Chakra:** Represents our foundation and feeling of being grounded.
   - **Location:** Base of spine in tailbone area.
   - **Emotional issues:** Survival issues such as financial independence, money, and food.

2. <u>**Sacral Chakra**</u>: Our connection and ability to accept others and new experiences.
   - **Location:** Lower abdomen, about 2 inches below the navel and 2 inches in.
   - **Emotional issues:** Sense of abundance, well-being, pleasure, sexuality.

DEVELOPPING SINCE MEETING MY MAN!

3. <u>**Solar Chakra**</u>: Our ability to be confident and in-control of our lives.
   - **Location:** Upper abdomen in the stomach area.
   - **Emotional issues:** Self-worth, self-confidence, self-esteem.

4. <u>**Heart Chakra**</u>: - Our ability to love.
   - **Location:** Centre of chest just above heart.
   - **Emotional issues:** Love, joy, inner peace.

NO PROBLEMS THERE FOR ME AT THE MOMENT, GOING STRONG!

5. <u>**Throat Chakra**</u>: - Our ability to communicate.
   - **Location:** Throat.
   - **Emotional issues:** Communication, self-expression of feelings, the truth.

6. <u>**Brow Chakra**</u>: - Our ability to focus on and see the big picture.
   - **Location:** Forehead between the eyes. (Also called the Third Eye)
   - **Emotional issues:** Intuition, imagination, wisdom, ability to think and make decisions.

GETTING STRONGER BY THE DAY

7. <u>Crown</u> Chakra: - The highest Chakra represents our ability to be fully connected spiritually.
   - **Location:** The very top of the head.
   - **Emotional issues:** Inner and outer beauty, our connection to spirituality, pure bliss.

A rather interesting point that Lise makes is that energy comes from many sources: water, air, food, and that (get this) even thoughts we think are a source of energy! Wow... that's food for thought! *'The more a person's thoughts are pure and true, less food he needs.'* This is quite astonishing, isn't it Mac?

Everything is made of energy and energy must be in balance!

I am so going to apply this principle to my thoughts, although to be honest, I am certainly witnessing a change in me, since Lise and Chris have come into my life, I have noticed that not only my body has changed (hello, I dropped more than a dress size and I am now a beautiful size 10 . . I do want to get to 8 though ☺) and I am feel much more positive. I love Lise and Chris for what they taught me so far . . .

And now ... the exercises, which have helped me a great deal through the changing process. I was hesitant at first, but look how far I got!

"Take a good look at your everyday life. Do you feel that you are depleting your own energy resources for others? Do you give them all your energy, having none left for yourself? If you do, it is because you are not giving freely, but have expectations.

You probably have difficulty asking for and receiving help from others, which creates stress and a sense of dissatisfaction in you."

I can't say no! Especially at work. God I hate my job! Last year the company had to make some redundancies and guess who had the task of telling people? Me? My boss is a coward; he does not want to get involved in such things. It was so awful; I like to make people happy! I even had to sack Angela, my boss' PA, a sweet woman in her 50's. Such a lovely lady, very committed to her job! I felt so uncomfortable having to do my boss's dirty job! That poor woman was devastated, we both ended up crying! I must/want to change career direction, but what? What else am I good at? Jamie always say that I can be great at anything I want to do, he believes that I am more of anartistic type and working in a corporate environment is not for me. Oh sweet Jamie, who I have not seen in days! I can hear him coming and going, but I never actually see him. I must send him a text later.

If this is occurring in your relationship with your children....
This does not apply to me! But it might apply to Millie soon ;) Marco has already asked her to marry him, he wants a big family, at least 4 children! But Millie is the real commitment phoebe! She told him that she is not ready yet. She thinks she will and I quote "fuck everything up" just like her parents did. She is scared! I must lend this book to her, although, I know what she will say, "oh another one of your mum's hippy dippy stuff!" She is very opinionated is Millie, but she has a good heart and she is beautiful! I love her!

_ If your energy is being depleted at work or with your mate, it is up to you to bring about change by openly discussing the matter with whoever is involved. Take care of yourself

regardless of what others may think of feel about it. You are doing it for yourself, but everyone around you will benefit.

Must change job, must look for another job . . . but not just yet, cos it is nice to see Chris everyday! OMG, look at my big grin reflecting on your screen Mac!

_Once you have understood how to increase and balance your energy in every area of life, proceed to the next chapter

I have understood that I need to keep my thoughts more pure and positive and change my job. That might not happen in a heartbeat, but I am committed Mac!

_ Here is your affirmation. Repeat as often as possible

I AM MORE CONSCIOUS OF MY GREAT ENERGY AND AM RELEARNING TO USE MORE WISELY.

JUST GOT A TEXT FROM CHRIS, "THANK YOU SEXY FOR BREAKFAST AND GREAT SEX!" (So polite! I paid for his breakfast, he is skint at the moment, poor chap! He does not make half of what I make and I am more than happy to help him out! And he did pay for the cinema the other night!)

Good night Mac, sweet dreams! x

Hello Mac

No Monday blues for this 'Sexy', that's how Chris calls me. I did not manage to speak to you him at all today as I was busy in meetings from the moment I sat at my desk until 5 pm; and Chris finishes work at 4.30. But the cutie did send me this e-mail, "Good morning Sexy, how are you today? Did you have sweet dreams of me? I did of you! Have a great day!" Oh God! My heart is beating so fast!

My energy is running so high in my body, I simply had to go for a run (well more like a jog!) along the river! Such a beautiful evening, I love, love, love London in the sun! That beautiful pink sunset light turned the clouds into pink fluffy cupcakes with red velvet frosting on top. Wait a minute, why am I thinking of cupcakes now? Of course, I have only had a round of toast with marmite all day! I forgot to eat all day! 'It must be love, love, love" ... I am in Love and life is getting better every day!

Well work is not so good, mind! The Boss announce that we have to downsize again! And guess who has to do a full report on who should go? And guess who has to do the nasty work of sacking people, again! Me! Oh I hate it! I mustn't get this affect this wonderful day I am having.

Millie and I are going to have a catch up with dinner and True Blood. We have not had a proper catch up in ages. Sadly Jamie won't be around, he is going to, get ready for this, the gym! This revelation came as a surprise to me. Jamie, the gym? Ever since I have known him he has always preferred booze over gym! I guess we all change . . .

No Lise no personal development exercises today, I just didn't get a chance and I do want to spend some time with my best friend tonight.

Catch up with you tomorrow Mac!

KX

Tuesday 19th May

Dear Mac

What a day, what a day! Working on the report has completely floored me, what kind of energy can I generate writing a report on who I think should lose their job! Millie says that it is just a job and I should not put any emotions in it, but it's difficult for me! She is such a strong person, she is a Leo, fiery, type A woman. Sometimes I wish I was more like that!

We even have to make cuts in Chris's department and of course I will do anything in my power for him to keep his job! He is so talented and I think he actually deserves a promotion.

He asked me out for a drink tonight - I can't wait - I need to take my mind off this awful day at work! He is such a sweetie, I told him about the report and knowing how hard it is for me, he wants to cheer me up and help me out if I need advice. What a sensitive, considerate and selfless young man, he wants to take on my burdens!

On a more positive note though, I jumped on the scale this morning and I am now 60 kilos! Now this is amazing, considering that I was £68 kilos 3 weeks ago!

I took a full hour lunch today and I read chapter 9 and did the exercises. It was not a really long chapter and I don't find that it applies to me as such. I am gonna share it with you and then get ready to meet my everything! Thankfully, I have already worked out what to wear on my way home this afternoon. Dark blue skinny jeans, pink long v neck T-shirt, black boyfriend jacket and white Converse! Casual but sexy as my boobs will be hugged and lifted by my bright pink Victoria Secrets push up bra! Oh and knickers are matching! Chris likes that! "Classy stuff" he says!

Now focus Kate, Chapter 9, 'Disease and Accidents'

"I don't know what the words 'disease' and 'accidents' mean to you, but most people seem to think they are the result of misfortune or bad luck; that they are manifestation of injustice in their lives, especially if the disease is 'hereditary' o contracted through someone else. This way of thinking is contradictory to the great Universal Law of Responsibility.

The concept of self-responsibility, when it pertains to accidents and disease, may seem a little extreme to you, but we cause them to happen unconsciously. That's why it is difficult to believe that we are thus responsible for them. An illness is simply a message sent to your body by your body. It is a signal given to you by your Superconscious mind, or your inner GOD, to tell you that something in the way you are thinking of behaving is going against the Great Universal Law of Love – the Law of Responsibility. To blame nature or to be angry when you become ill is senseless. Instead, be open to the message that your body is giving you and thank ROUMA for it. When you do not completely understand what it is telling you, ask it for guidance – for clarification – so that you can understand the message and accept it fully and find the peace of mind you will need to heal yourself. Accept your inner GOD."

Therefore, when we feel ill or we suffer physical pain, we should not complain about it, but we should take responsibility and ask our best friend, our body, why? What is wrong? Pain is not simply a physical manifestation, but it is also a metaphysical (beyond the physical) message.

The book gives a full alphabetical list of common illnesses and their metaphysical causes. Those that apply to me are:

Backache and Cellulite. And here is their metaphysical explanation.

"Any problems in the area of the back are an indication that you feel you are carrying 'the weight of the world on your back'. You feel that you have no support and that you are responsible for the happiness or misery of all your loved ones. Your Superconscious mind is sending you the following message: "Stop thinking you are responsible for everyone else. If you want to give others support, don't do it out of a sense of obligation, but of your own free will." Take responsibility for your own decisions – you will be able to handle them.

When a person feels he is lacking support from others, he wants it, but usually will not allow them to give it to them out of pride. Eventually others become discouraged and no longer offer further assistance.

If your pain is in the UPPER BACK, it is related to lack of support from others. LOWER BACK pain is an indication of lack of material or monetary support."

I always have tense shoulders, neck and my upper back aches on a daily basis. I have gotten so used to it that sometimes I forget it is there. But on days like today I can feel it all right! I now understand why!

As for Cellulite …effing cottage cheese on my thighs, I feel so ashamed of it. In summer I can never bare my legs, it is so daunting, I hate it, probably more than I hate my job!

Lise does not provide an explanation in book, but I have done a google search and this is what I found:

'CELLULITE: Not appreciating one's own body. Issues about your sexuality. Liver metabolism problems.' (http://www.galaxyhealing. com.au/articles/metaphysicsart.html).

I REST MY CASE!

The exercise at the end of the chapter are the following:

- **Draw up a list of all your current physical discomforts.** See above
- **Thank your body for sending you signals regarding these discomforts and ask your superconscious mind what their meaning is.** Thank you Cellulite for delivering to me the message that I don't like myself!
- **Take care of at least one of these discomforts. Take the smallest one, if you wish, and make it disappear! Having done so, you will understand the correlation between the physical and the metaphysical.** CELLULITE! DISAPPEAR PLEASE! NOW!

- Repeat this affirmation as often as possible and go on to the next chapter

I TRUST MY BODY, WHO IS MY GUIDE AND MY GREATEST FRIEND, MORE AND MORE EACH DAY, IN DOING SO, I REGAIN PEACE, HEALTH, LOVE AND HARMONY.

There you have it Mac, all done, I am off to my date . . . I am so happy to have Chris in my life, I am so grateful he is looking after me tonight! I wonder if he has noticed my cellulite? I always ensure to switch off the lights when we do it, make love that is! Can you feel cellulite?

Good Night Mac

X

Wednesday 20th May

Dear Mac

I had the most amazing night last night! Chris told me 'I LOVE YOU'! I did not sleep all night, well you know, we entertained each other in other ways! He fell asleep straight after sex, I could not! I kept staring at the ceiling with a giant Cheshire cat smile stamped on my face! I am still so high! High on life! So in love with life. **LOVE**

We met in Pitcher and Piano in St Pauls, he got there before me and grabbed us a table. He as looking a glorious as ever. Although the bar was quite dark, his piercing blue eyes were shining bright. He was sitting there in his leather biker jacket, baby blue V neck jumper and dark blue jeans! He was wearing white Converse too; we are a match made in heaven!

A big glass of Pinot Grigio was already waiting for me, he knows we so well! And when he saw me he stood up, gave me an electric big hug and kissed me on the lips

C: How is it going?

Me: Good thank you. You?

C: I have been worried about you today (so sweet!), you looked pretty tormented in the office today and I am here to help you, you can rely on me you know?

Me: Oh Chris, Thank you, I appreciate it, but really it's not your problem and I don't want to burden you with work stuff.

C: Sexy, (love it when he calls me that), we are a couple, I am your boyfriend (are we?? My heart skipped a beat!)

I was taken aback by the word boyfriend, I burst into a stupid little nervous laughter

Me: Are you now? Does that mean that I am your girlfriend? (I stopped breathing as I was waiting for his answer)

C: You are funny! Of course you are sexy. Why? are you dating somebody else? I sure hope not, you would break my heart, I love you!

My heart did not skip a beat this time. I literally died and went to heaven for a good 10 seconds… I was speechless, I swear my mouth dropped open. I gulped down what was left of my wine, the adrenaline was running wild in my body, I froze, but I managed to smile! Panic central mixed with total joy!

He obviously noticed the shock on my face and kissed me, the most perfect kiss!

C: Do you not feel the same way?

Me: Oh my God! Of course Chris! I am just in shock, you know I am a very bashful, but I am so happy!

(I felt this way since the first time I saw you! Did not say this to him to appear cool). At this point a needed a stiff drink, this was the first time ever a guy said the L word to me!

My life is amazing; Hello!? A sex god like Chris is in LOVE with me!?

We kissed again and it was even more perfect than the previous one! It was such a Hollywood moment! And trust me Mac, I never thought it could be possible to top the previous passion but we did.

Chris is making me change for the better, he really helped me make sense of my work task, the infamous report. He even offered his opinion and shared his opinion on who should go and why. It totally made sense. I took his advice. Unprofessionally I thought to get rid of Stephanie, you know the office bitch, but he made me see how she was a positive asset to the team. I was reluctant and a little jealous, but I he said that I should act professionally and should not let my personal feelings get involved.

This morning I completed the report and handed it in to my boss. I do not want to think about it anymore, it's done. Chris thinks I am too nice and in my job I need to get a tougher skin and make bold decisions. 'You need to think less about others' feelings be less emotional'. He is right, I need to grow a pair really! No More Miss Nice! Tell that to my anxiety though. It's like I have hideous brown moths in my chest and they are slowly chewing my heart! Anxiety is a BITCH! Nothing that some Kalms pills will not sort out though.

I have not managed to go any further with my book today, but I am now going to go for a jog and will read the next chapter tonight.

Oh text.... 'Well done sexy, I am proud of you!' He is so sweet...he is proud that I took his advice and handed in the report!

A' tomorrow Mac!

Thursday 21st May

Hello Mac!

Another amazing day in my loved up world! I have to say it is great that I now have a boyfriend, my friends have totally deserted me!

Millie is spending all her time with Marco, she actually left this morning for a romantic weekend in Rome (Nice!), Jamie... I don't even know what he looks like these days, I have not seen him in ages... Millie said that she had a quick catch up with him the other day and that he is looking pretty good. I am baffled, I am not ouie what she meant. She reckons he has a girlfriend (?). I really miss him though, I would like to tell him all about my life and Chris, but he does not seem to be interested, maybe he has a girlfriend? It is often the case with people who are loved up to change their appearance and disappear from the face of the earth! I will send him an e-mail tomorrow . . .

Meanwhile . . . as it seems that I have the whole flat to myself, I have arranged a romantic dinner here for Chris! This is what is on the menu, steak and chips (his favourite!) with steamed vegetables and sugar free Eaton Mess (his favourite desserts!). He actually ordered the whole menu! I think it is great that he tells me what he wants as opposed to having to guess. It avoids me making any sort of mistakes . . . I really want to impress him and we know how food is the way to a man's heart!

Me cooking steak is going to be interesting though, this the first time I have ever cooked meat and thank goodness for the world wide web, found the recipe … it's actually quite easy. I also found a recipe for black pepper sauce to accompany the steak as it seems that the steak on its own is a bit boring! Who knew?

But before I get going with the cooking, which will really not take me so long . . . I want to share with you the best bits of Chapter 10, 'Food for Thought', how appropriate !

'The human body knows instinctively, from the point of conception, what it requirements are. It does not have to be taught how to sleep, be thirsty or hungry, cry, cough, perspire, be warm or cold, eliminate, digest, yawn, vomit, swallow, laugh, move, bleed or heal itself. Somehow, in the process of maturation, we've forgotten to trust our instincts. …

There is an interesting correlation between our eating and drinking patterns and the way we lead our everyday lives. ...

If you discover that you are someone who has many eating habits, you may also notice that you are the kind of person who is very concerned with what others think, do or say about you. Instead of thinking, acting or dressing in a way that pleases you, especially if it is considered "unusual", you tend to be more concerned about the reaction of others and will conform so that you do not initiate any kind of negative response. Worrying about such insignificant things can be draining on your energy and will create an underlying dissatisfaction inside you. Learn how to be conscious of your real needs. ... Get in touch with what YOU need inside to make your life a success!'

I know I say this often, but does Lise know me? I feel like she is addressing me personally when I read her lines ... maybe my issues are common to other women? I am ashamed of saying it, but yes, I am always so concerned with what others might think of me, I hate confrontation and I just want to be invisible most of the time!!! Please don't judge me Mac!

Like most women, I am an emotional eater, that I know! That's why I am fat, or rather, I used to be fat. Love has healed me. It is really interesting how as I feel loved by the most gorgeous man on the planet, I heal and I go from ugly duckling to a swan (OK, almost a swan!). I am still no way near as perfect as I would like to be for him! Girls look at him and that makes me feel insecure. There are gorgeous women out there and he can have his pick! His flirting with Stephanie in the office bothers me a lot, well she flirts, she is gorgeous and he is a man ... Anyhow, I don't want to get down on myself, there must be something good about me if Chris loves me there must be something good about me! Either that or he is blind, or he is one of those men, who have ugly girlfriends so that they will not be cheated on???

'You see, you need never worry about whether you are getting enough food or the right kind of food, if you learn to listen to your body. Trust it to tell you exactly what you need and when you need it. Never eat when you are not hungry '"in case you don't get a change to eat on time..." *Wait for the signal from your body – it will tell you what is required in terms of nutrition when a deficiency is indicated (i.e. iron, calcium, protein, fat, sugar, etc.) it will ensure that you have a taste for precisely the food that will balance you. Your brain, the ultimate computer, has registered the chemical make-up of every food you have ever tasted and knows what to prescribe.'*

This is another level of trust, I have never thought of this. I have always thought that our bodies are something we need to train. That they are basically flawed and that we need to whip them into shape. Some people are born with the lucky genes and look like models (see Chris, Stephanie and Millie) and then there are those like me, gorilla lookalikes. Hairs and fat cells out of control! Am I really responsible for the way I look? Can I really learn to trust my body? Should I not count calories? Should I not go for runs so I can burn the morning croissant? This kind of stuff makes my anxiety flair up!

I know I am an obsessive dieter. I try all sort of diets. Pick up a magazine and try it. After all if it works for celebrities, why would it not work for me? Well they sort of do and don't. I lose weight for a week, if I can stick with it and then put the weight back on and sometimes more. I guess I could be called YO- YO dieter? Shit! I am a mess!

'As you increase your level of awareness, it will be easier to recognize and interpret your body's message and act accordingly. Do your share and your body will do its share. In this way, your energy will become balance and more evenly distributed. Being in harmony ensures good health. ...

Many people continue to use certain ingredients in their daily diet that do not provide nutrition for the body and only cause the loss of energy. Among these poisons are alcohol, white sugar (and other refined foods such as white flour, white rice and white bread), caffeine, salt, tobacco an all chemicals (medicine, drugs, preservatives and colourings) as well as non essential fats. There are many good books on nutrition available on the market. I would suggest you consult your local library or bookstore, if you are interested in investigating the subject of nutrition further.'

OMG, what fun would life be without alcohol? Sugar? Pizza? I can I wake up without my morning coffee? Seriously Lise? Come on, what kind of boring life does she lead?

'If you force your body to ingest alcohol, soft drinks, sweets and chemicals, it is a signal that you do not like yourself very much. Don't be surprised when your body can not do what you ask of it and you are robbed of energy. Your body is your best friend – you are in this together. Treat it accordingly.'

More emoji bombs exploding in my head!

Is this the reason why I have so much cellulite on my legs then? I think liposuction could be a quicker solution for me. I cannot conceive a life without alcohol, sugar, coffee ... Maybe I can cut down. But I don't think I can cut out!

I think Chris loves his body a lot. He is very good with his food and since we have been going out I have been drinking less wine and I don't have the compulsion to eat as much ice cream I used to. I just don't feel the need for it, he is now the sugar of my life.

'Craving sugar is an indication that you lack sweetness in your life, you do not allow yourself things that would please you and when you do, you feel guilty.

Cravings for salty foods indicate a critical, judgmental personality. You are probably your own worst critic.

Cravings for spicy food, your life is probably blander that you would like

Caffeine cravings indicate a need for stimulation on a psychological level'

I crave all of them at some point in the day!!! Seriously, I am a hot mess, how can Chris love me?

Exercise for Chapter 1.

'Every day, ask yourself if you are really hungry before eating of drinking anything and ask your body if it is what it needs. At the end of the each day, write down what you were feeling and what was going on at each meal, or snack – did you eat out of hunger, habit or for emotional reasons? This exercise is not for the purpose of creating a "diet plan", but to help you become more aware of what dominates your life – what part of your life needs to be more balanced – the physical, the mental or the emotional. Once you have determined this, you will find you

are more in tune with the needs of your body and better able to provide them.'

This will be a good exercise for me. It will be good for me to keep track of what I eat and really get in tune with my body. Perfections requires self- inspection ... I just made this up ;)

Affirmation:

I AM MORE AND MORE ALERT AND CONSCIOUS OF WHAT MOTIVATES MY WAY OF EATING AND I NOW WAIT FOR MY BODY TO LET ME KNOW WHAT IT NEEDS AND WHEN IT IS HUNGRY.

I feel good about this chapter, I think I have learned a little more about myself and I am determined to discover more. Who knows I might get down to a size 8!

Now is cooking and dinner with my everything!

Wish me luck Mac!

K x

Friday 22nd May

Hi Mac!

I took a duvet day today! Dinner with Chris was amazing. He brought a DVD - another Bond Movie, which I am starting to quite enjoy! I think!? These films are jammed packed with action and they are very entertaining! Chris says that James Bond is not chauvinistic, he just very charismatic. Maybe? He might have a point?

We end up drinking 2 bottles of wine! I did downed most of it, so much for not poisoning my body! But I just feel so nervous around him and wine relaxes me. My body issues disappear when I drink and I can enjoy sex a lot more! Needless to say, sex was hot! But I will not go into any details as I don't remember the details ... but it was hot! What else to expect Mac?!

And this morning he asked me to take a duvet day and make him breakfast. It's not like it was an order. 'I think you should take a duvet day and make me breakfast, you have had a stressful week, and deserve a long weekend! I would love a full English, you don't mind making some food, do you? You are so good at it! I would take you out, but I am skint! This job pays peanuts!'

You see he thinks of me all the time, so sweet! And he is absolutely right, he deserves a better job, a job where he feels valued and is paid a hell of a lot more!

I have never taken a duvet day and although I feel super guilty about it now, I am kind of happy that I did it, I feel naughty, sexy and empowered! What is he doing to me?

I quickly popped to Tesco's and got us eggs, bacon, sausages, ketchup and beans. Full English breakfast for my love! YouTube came to the rescue again as I don't know how to cook meat!

After breakfast he took a shower and left. He took a duvet day too, he did not need to call anyone, I guess those are the perks of going out with the HR manager! ☺

I will not be seeing tonight as he has a stag do. His best friend is getting married next month. He has not yet asked me to be his + one, I think he was a little hangover from last night. But I think I ought to plan what to wear, and start beautifying, just in case! He will ask me to be his plus one, what do you think Mac? Why do I always doubt myself and others? He loves me, naturally he would to show me off to his friends!?

So it's now 2 pm, I am alone in my flat, got to do something to entertain myself! Thank God for my book. Although Lise writes in her book not to move to chapter 11 after a week of reading chapter 10, I can't wait that long . . .

But first a shower, a jog along South Bank and then back to Lise.

And tomorrow my Cake Designing course! Have I mentioned that I booked it for tomorrow? I can't wait. Hopefully I will learn a lot and make some new friends. I feel incredibly lonely when Chris leaves. Millie is away, Jamie, I don't know what is going on with him! He is gone completely AWOL! I 'll text and see if he fancies a drink tonight.

Shower now . . .although I still smell of Chris' aftershave and I don't want to wash it off!

Oh What a glorious day in London Town! I went for a jog along the river, wore a baseball cap and sunglasses, just like celebrities do when they don't want to be noticed. HR manager takes a duvet day and gets found out whilst jogging along the river Themes! This Being Naughty stuff makes me feel paranoid and guilty, definitely not liberated! When am I going to learn to be cool?

The sun was shining kissing my skin, whilst a slight breeze kept me cool. I sweat buckets, it's quite disgusting...I sweat like a man, why has Mother Nature been so unkind to me? Most women have this healthy glow after exercising, I look ridiculously flustered!

I was listening to my music, enjoying myself and then ... I started to obsess . . . 'why has he not yet invited me to his best friend's wedding? Why does he take so long to text me back? Why has he not yet introduced me to his friends? Why does he want to keep our relationship a secret in the office? Why has he not updated his Facebook status to 'in relationship'? Am I sexy enough for him? Smart enough? Come to think of it, I really don't know much about him and he does not know much about me. We love each other, we have amazing sex, but what about intimacy? Too soon too much? Relationships are hard! Bloody hard if you ask me!

Jamie texted me back and he said he is free to catch up with me this eve. I can't wait to see him tonight. I miss him. He suggested we go to this raw vegan food restaurant near Old street. What on earth is raw food? He loves his burgers and chips? Something is definitely up with him!

Speaking of food, I still have not had anything to eat since this morning... I must be high on life! My higher self must be totally satisfied with all the love it's/I am getting!

Chapter 11 is called 'Ideal weight', how appropriate. I jumped on the scales this morning and I am now 58kg. I cannot wait to get to 52Kg!

'In discussing weight problems, both overweight and underweight are equally important issues.' I am going to skip straight to why one is overweight …

'…-being too heavy, or gaining weight too easily – indicates several things. When someone "goes on a diet", he shows a fundamental lack of responsibility in his life. He wants to alter the effect without determining the cause. Success from dieting is only an illusion; this is why it is usually only temporary (statistics indicate a 98% failure rate of permanent success). The body reacts when it is mistreated. Most people gain back more than they have lost.'

I hope this does not apply to my love diet!

'Remember that your body, through your Superconscious mind, is your best friend. It communicates with you in many ways. Instead of thanking it, you rebel; you want to change it because it does not coincide with the image you want to project. By communicating with your body, you will get to the root of the problem and with loss will become a simple and healthy process. … As you change your way of thinking, the rest will follow. … To circumvent any problem, it is best to eat when hungry and to stop eating when comfortably full. This practice alone would induce weight loss. Listen to your body – you will receive all the signals you need. Act on them'

Aw, if only life was that easy Lise!

'Excess weight may indicate a lack of acceptance or lack of love of oneself. You feel unlovable, unworthy, and crave the acceptance and love of others.'

I can see what she means. I never really thought of it, but as I read these lines, it becomes quiet clear and it make me feel quite sad.

I always put others before me. I am a people pleaser, I do not like confrontation in the slightest. I like to blend in the background as supposed to be noticed. Is that such a bad thing? I feel safe, I want people to leave me alone!

As a child a was bullied because for being a vegetarian and I wore second hand clothes. My mum has always been too busy saving the world than thinking about my feelings. That's why I now want to blend in, don't express my opinion as I don't want to be picked on! I guess I have developed this way of being to protect myself.

There is also the fact that when I lived my Italian grandparents, I got fed lots and lots of amazing food! Perhaps had I been more active and taken up some kind of sport or dance, I could have burnt it all off. Yes, but I was too shy to find myself in a class with other girls, who were slender and wearing the latest fashion; too humiliating.

But that's the past now and I don't want to sound like a drama queen ☺ I am much better now, I am shedding the weight and I have a boyfriend and he is GORGEOUS! Maybe I should take Chris to one of my school reunions and show him off. What is it that they say? 'Vengeance is a dish served cold!'

So ... Self love, acceptance and no dieting = weight loss! I will work on it, although, I am still not sure how to love myself ...

Let's see if the exercises will help.

-   **Make a list of all the foods you deprive yourself of presently. On the list, include the foods you would like to eat or drink but don't dare to for fear of putting on weight. Acknowledge that there is part of you that is still "on a diet"**

HELL YEAH! I am always on a diet! I was a chubby kid, and I think I must have been that way cos of lack of parenting. But I have already said that and I have also forgiven them for it. Let's face it, as a single lonely child you never get to share cakes and biscuits! So it's Not my fault!

And I must have been 12 when I started dieting, I remember my first attempt at it was to starve myself for the whole day and only have dinner in the evening. It worked, I dropped more than a stone. I stopped eating cakes and became obsessed with calorie counting. This obsession continues, I pretty much know all the calories I consume! Ice cream is my guilty pleasure or maybe a plain obsession!

The list of things I deprive myself when I am on a diet and when I am not drunk! Bread, pasta, chocolate, biscuits, crisps, cheese, ice cream, … anything too fatty, I always go for the low fat, low carb = no taste option!

When I am drunk, anything goes! Yes when I love myself ☺

But I must come clean about something Mac. I do occasionally binge too. I am ashamed of it, nobody knows, not even Millie and Jamie. I binge on the exact same foods I deprive myself of. I guess strict diets can take you there!

- **Accept the idea that you can eat what you want and when you want. IT IS YOUR BODY. You do not owe an explanation to anyone but yourself.**

Hard Lise, Hard! I actually quite disgust myself when I binge eat. Sometimes my hormones are out of control and I just don't seem to stop. Carbs, sugar, carbs. I have been on a diet for almost 20 years!

18 to be precise! I turn 30 next month – and I wonder if Chris has already planned anything special for me! - I just wasn't blessed with the slim gene. Nonetheless, I will give it a good go, starting from tomorrow. I am sure that the cake designing course will give me ample opportunity to try out my sweet treats! I am scared!

- **Begin to listen carefully to what your body is telling you that it needs. Try to be aware of any 'cravings' you experience and determine the basis. Before you eat anything, ask yourself if you are really hungry and if that particular food is beneficial to your body. Eat consciously.**

Again, so hard!! Surely If I give into my cravings I would be obese and Chris will dump me! How frightening! Asking myself if I am really hungry will certainly be a first for me. I generally eat because it is time to eat, I never question if I am hungry, I just assume I must be . . . Interesting . . .

- **Remember that programming yourself with "cannot" and "should not", will only cause obsession and will push you to achieving the opposite of what you want to achieve.**

My life is a constant, I should not, I must not, I should, I must . . . Must change that!

- **Repeat this affirmation as often as you can and go the next chapter.**

I ACCEPT MYSELF AS I AM RIGHT NOW. MY GREAT INNER STRENGHT IS HELPING ME REACH AND MAINTAN MY IDEAL WEIGHT.

Feel very good after reading this chapter, I feel like I got to understand part of me, which I never even considered. I have never thought about questioning why I eat what I eat and when I eat. Good one Lise

Now I am going to get ready for my Raw-Food experience with Jamie. Not sure about the food, but I can't wait to see Jamie.

Saturday 23rd May

A great night overall! I had a lovely catch up with Jamie followed by Chris' text: 'Miss you sexy! I will be at yours in half hour. I want to punish you naughty girl!' I wonder what makes him think that I am a naughty girl?

When he got to my place he passed out on the bed. I literally spent an hour watching him sleep ... he so cute when he sleeps, his vulnerable side shines through!

We did have sex this morning though! And it is 3 pm and he still sleeping in my bed. Well I made him some breakfast and then he went back to sleep.

I missed my cake designing course, but it's ok, I much prefer to spend time with my love than learning how to make cakes! He is more important. I can always do the course another time! And anyway I bought is through Living Social ... no big deal! Love comes first, relationships are all about compromise. Aren't they?

Last night with Jamie was lovely and OMG, he has changed so much, I almost did not recognize him!

He looked half his size, his face looked fresh, smooth, spot free and he got himself some rather trendy haircut. And it wasn't just his looks that have changed, his aura, energy was so confident and calm. He has always been confident and clam to me, but there was something different about him and I can't even describe it. His clothes were different too, gone were the baggy jeans and shirt. He was wearing much tighter dark blue jeans, gray sweater and black boots. He almost looked like and Abercrombie model! I had never realized that a handsome man was hiding in my friend Jamie!

J: Hello gorgeous

Me: hello stranger, I have not seen you in ages

Big hug, it felt so good, warm and familiar

J: How are you Kate? You look great, I almost did not recognize you!

Me: Me? What about you Jamie, you look so different! So good

Waitress comes to the table: 'Can I get you guys anything to drink?'

J: Pinot Grigio Kate?

Me: Yes please (he knows me so well)

Waitress: 'What about you?' she flashes a big flirtatious smile at him and pushes her boobs forward!

J: I will have a glass of biodynamic red please. – I think he said biodynamic, don't even ask me what that means-!

Waitress: Sure, I will be right back with those drinks for you. – Smiling at Jamie and not even acknowledging my presence.

It's pretty much what I get when I am out with Chris. It's like I am invisible to these women! I am a lucky woman! Women want my men ☺

Me: I can't believe that we live in the same house and that we have not seen each other in so long. What happened, we used to be so close? And look at you! Don't take this the wrong way, when did you get so handsome? Do you have a girlfriend?

Waitress comes back. 'Here you go', beaming smile at Jamie and I swear those boobs where pushed a little more up. They were almost in her month! 'Are you ready to order your food?'

Jamie is a true gentleman, he smiled back, said thank you and asked her to give us a few more minutes.

J: No girlfriend. At the risk of sounding like a girl, I am working on myself. I took a good look at myself. You know how I disliked looking at myself in the mirror? Well I had to face it and become brave. My life is changing. Somebody at works suggested I take up hot yoga. I was dubious at first, but I went along to a class and I have been going every day since!

Emoji bombs exploding in my head!

Me: Yoga? Every day? Is that what it does to you? - I thought to myself, is that what it does to you? Turns you from an ugly duckling into a swan? – No girl? Are you sure? Your clothes are so great! I didn't know you had style? What about this restaurant? Raw food? I mean, look at you? You look terrific!

J: Thank you Kate, - he says blushing, yes men blush too! Yoga, meditation, mindfulness are helping me to understand and accept myself for who I am. The more you accept yourself, the more confident in your skin you get and changes just happen from there.

Me: I must try some of this yoga myself. I do Pilates and jogging, but maybe I should give yoga a go too. (maybe that's how I will learn to love myself?)

J: sure, I can give you the details of the studio where I go. But enough about me, what about you? I have been so busy; I don't know what is going on in your life. Are you still seeing that guy from the Drunken Monkey?

It dawned on me that I had not seen Jamie for almost a month, I can't believe it has been that long.

Me: Chris? Yes, and we are in love! – it just escaped my mouth!

Jamie lowered his gaze to the menu and said 'That's great; I think we better choose the food'

Me: This is a completely new experience for me, can you help me out?

J: I have been here a few times and I recommend the 'pad Thai', I know you like Thai food and although this is not your usual Pad Thai, I think you will like it. But for starters we should share a cheese board. It's not made of cheese, it's made of nuts and the flavours are really quite interesting.

Me: I trust your judgment. By the Way, I am no longer a vegetarian! Chris made me see the light, I was a vegetarian because of somebody else's rules, my mum's!

J: mmm interesting, I am now a vegan!

Me: seriously? You? What? You loved your meat sooo much! Did you do it to lose weight?

J: Well not really, I am doing it because I care for myself and what goes on inside my body.

Me: That's lovely Jamie, I am so happy to hear that you care for yourself. I am reading this book at the moment, self-help book - I feel like I can talk to Jamie about everything and I know he will not judge me! I have not told Chris about the book as I think he is way too manly to understand something like that. Jamie is not at all girly, but he is more in touch with his feminine side and he does not judge me. With Chris I want to be perfect, with Jamie, I can relax and be flawed Kate, The Gorilla with cellulite! – It's mostly about the relationship with ourselves, energy that our thoughts create and it gives lots of exercises to work on these issues.

I truly feel that my life is changing and for the better

Waitress: 'Would you like to order?'

J: Can you please bring us the cheese board to share as a starter and 2 Pad Thais. Thank you. – You were saying

Me: I feel happier with myself, as you can see I have lost weight, I am in love with the most gorgeous guy, he loves me, I have learnt how to make bold decisions in my job. I feel better about myself. Chris has a lot to do with it too. He is making me see the other side of things, he is making me a stronger person.

J: good for you Kate! You certainly look great! And what about baking, have you done much so far? Did you end up booking that cake design course? You are so good at making cakes!

Me: no time really – did not want to tell him that I missed the course, feel somehow guilty? - have been very busy. Besides, when you are in love you don't need sweets

J: You are very talented Kate, I think you should keep it up, stay open to new things! Speaking of new things, I am off to New York, I have signed up for an intensive photography course.

Me: what? New York? Why do you have to go all the way there? What about your job?

J: Kate, you know I always loved photography,

Me: yeah I know! I lost count of how many photography exhibitions you have taken me to!

J smiles: I have decided to turn it from a hobby into something professional. New York has renowned photography schools. The course is 6 months long, intensive. Work is fine with it; I am taking an unpaid sabbatical. I already have a place where I can stay!

Me: Sounds like you have it all planned out! Does Millie know?

J: She does, she is super excited and I am actually renting her flat.

I felt a pang of jealousy, Millie has not mentioned anything? Why?

Me: I am happy for you, but I am so going to miss you. 6 months! Promise you will come back!

J: I will and you can always come and visit!? We could Skype, e-mail, What's App ...Technology is on our side!

We had our food, it was shockingly nice, I felt stuffed, but light. I truly had a lovely time with Jamie, he is has such a calming influence on me, I will miss him a lot whilst he is away. 6 Months!

After dinner, I came home and he went to meet some of his yoga friends. He invited me to join them, but Chris had just texted me and I run home to get all ready for him.

I will miss Jamie ... but I will go to visit for sure, I have always wanted to go to NYC and do the Sex and the City tours. My favourite show of all times!

... ...

3 hours later

Sadly Chris never made it to mine and he didn't even bother to return my calls or texts. I am very worried, London can be a very dangerous city, anything can happen.

Men can be so selfish! I could have had a night out with Jamie and instead I am here, home alone! I have already managed to wolf down a Ben and Jerry Cherry Garcia topped with 2 vodka shots.

I am so agitated and worried! I think there is a pizza in the freezer, I am going to have that with extra cheese topping ... I don't care that I had dinner a few hours ago! My name is Kate Arnold and I am an emotional eater!

Sunday 24th May

Good morning Mac

Profuse apologies for how I behaved last night, I was feeling sorry for myself. I am good now! Chris sent me a lovely text 'Love you Sexy, I will swing by later on if you have any food going?' He really does enjoy my food. I think I will treat him to a Sunday roast ☺. Never made it before, so YouTube to the rescue.

This is what I love about my relationship with Chris, he pushes me out of my comfort zone, I am always pushing the boundaries! 'That's where real growth happens' Chris says all the time!

This would also be my first Sunday roast since becoming a meat eater, I think I am going to stay safe and do chicken! It is the second time in my entire life that I eat chicken. It really does not taste of much. It does taste exactly like Quorn mind you.

I have not yet told my mum that I eat meat. Who knows what she might say. 'Animals are our friends, we don't eat our friends'. The more I think about it and the more I think that she is a food fascist and that she should have exposed me to eating meat. Thanks to Chris, I am discovering the real me! The me that cooks and eats meat, because guess what Mum, it is natural and I don't need to follow your rules. Except of course that I am reading the book she suggested and I must admit, it is a good suggestion!

I have not spoken to her in ages, she called me a few times, but I did not pick up. Just texted her back 'I am fine Mum, busy now, will call you soon'. I am doing all this work on myself and I am trying the break the ties, so when I feel strong enough in myself I will call her! I have totally forgiven her, but I don't want to talk to her right now.

I better be off now Mac, lots to do, food and shave my legs! Again!

BTW – diet is back on track. I have only had a black coffee this morning. I think I am still digesting that pizza, ice cream and wine. Everything was rather large size. I felt so ashamed of myself for eating and drink all that last night, but today I am going to be good.

… … …

Hi Mac, me again …

Sunday dinner was a great success, I actually ended up cooking Pork for the first time. Not my favourite meat, but Chris loved it. I had some of the roast potatoes, broccoli, carrots and peas with gravy. So far I have tried beef, pork, chicken and I can't really say that they are my most favourite foods in the world, it still feels strange, but as Chris say, I just need to get used to it.

Chris was so hangover today, he could barely speak, he asked me: 'do you mind if we don't chat much today, my head is hurting and I just want to enjoy this food and watch some football'. Bless him, I can sympathize, when you feel delicate the last thing you want to do is to make conversation. He ate his food, which he absolutely loved, and then moved the sofa to watch football. He was so knackered he fell asleep and I put a blanket over him, he looked so angelic, so beautiful, I cannot believe he is with me.

Anyhow, whilst he was watching the football/slept, I read Chapter 12, 'Sexuality'!!! I couldn't help but blushing as I was reading, and getting hot, whilst he head was resting on my legs whilst he was resting. Sooo sweet!

He slept for about 1 hour and when he woke he went straight home. He said he had quite a heavy weekend and thanked me for being such a great sexy nurse and for providing such good food. 'I will see you tomorrow sexy'.

I miss him when he is gone!

'Sexuality has always been a delicate topic' – You can say that again Lise! *'it is a difficult and complicated subject. Our sexuality is primal and fundamental to our very being. Through our sexuality, we have the potential to express our innermost selves and this element alone causes most people a great deal of discomfort.'*

I have always had a bit of a strange love/hate relationship with sexuality. I always feel uncomfortable getting naked, I keep wondering what I look like in some positions . . . Pinot Grigio always helps though. I am often drunk (well that was before Chris, LBC – Life Before Chris!) before I engage in a sexual act! Once Pinot Grigio kicks in, I let myself go and I really enjoy sex! I think as I don't remember much about it the day after …

'From generation to generation we have retained the fears and guilt associated with the word "sex". It wasn't long ago that "sex" was still

synonymous with the word "sin". As I write this, my Mum words come to mind 'sex is a beautiful thing! Sex and love make 2 people come together!' and sadly I caught her and my dad a few times coming together! Yuck, I think that's where my problems with sex come from!

'*The sexual act is the physical expression of the greatest possible fusion- that being the fusion of the Soul and the Sprit '–???* – '*A human being's fundamental purpose lies in achieving the fusion of his lower body with his higher body. This is why the sexual act is such a large issue. The Soul has profound need to reach the fusion with the Spirit – an act that culminates in profound bliss.*'

And I am pretty sure that Lise is referring to the BIG O? I am very ashamed of admitting it Mac, but I have no idea what the BIG O feels like. Sure sex with Chris is amazing, but I think I am still too self-conscious, or something like that. So I have to fake it ☹. I want to be perfect for him, I can't exactly make him feel like it is fault? Nonetheless, I am totally satisfied with my sex life!

I always thought that "sex" or "making love" were purely an animalistic act with feelings stirred in, I never realized it was concerned with spirituality, the fusion of soul and spirit?

According to Lise this is the reason why we have such great expectations of the sexual act, there is a much deeper level we are seeking to satisfy.

You know when you watch romantic films and they say that relationships based on purely on sex don't last? Well Lise agrees, she says '*a relationship based solely on sex is deprived of a solid base. The longer a couple develops a friendship prior to engaging in sexual intercourse, the more solid the relationship will be*'. Is she referring to the "rules" I certainly feel that I have known Chris for a long time before we had sex. And our relationship is most definitely not purely based on sex. Sadly though, I still have not met any of his friends or his parents for that matter, and at work nobody knows about our love. He says he wants to keep me all to himself and nobody needs to know our business. He is reserved and I so love him for it!

'This sexual repression has been transmitted through the generations and girls usually have more guilty feelings related to sex. Sexual taboos exist at the unconscious level and we must work the out in order for us to find inner peace.'

I have never linked sexuality with inner peace. There are so many ideas I am just not aware of. Maybe they should teach 'Self-Love' in schools!

And what about the Oedipus theory?! A rather obvious topic when talking about sexuality! If the Oedipus complex is not properly solved, this can cause sexual problems in adulthood!

'The Oedipus theory comes into play when a child is between there and six years of age. At this stage, children are becoming aware of their sexual energy: the little boy falls in love with his mother and the little girl with her father on all levels, including the physical. The little boy may become jealous of his father – a part of him admires his father but, on the other hand, he wants to take his father's place beside his mother. He feels caught between these two conflicting sets of feelings. Allowing a little boy to continue to sleep with his other at this stage can be confusing for him. It is time to gently explain that he is "bigger boy now, that he has his own room and that the parents have theirs ...

A little girl at this stage may also exhibit very sensual behaviours toward her father. She kisses and caresses him frequently and will interfere if he pays too much attention to her mother. – I feel a little uncomfortable writing this down! *– This stage is normal and healthy, but must be dealt with carefully, without discouraging normal development. I strongly encourage parents to talk to their children openly about what is happening to them, without giving too much detail. Children understand more than we give them credit for.'*

Comforting to know that this complex gradually disappears as the child nears six year of age! I must say, I really don't think I have ever suffered, or if I had I don't remember and frankly I don't want to. Thinking about me being in love with my dad as a little girl … mmm no, I am just going to move on, I am just not interested in incest and all of that. I don't see how learning causes behind them will improve my life. Disgusting! So I am going to skip straight to the exercises. Disgusting!

Although sexuality is an uncomfortable topic, I am going to spend some time doing the exercises as I want to experience a deeper connection with Chris and hopefully become a better lover ;)

- **Examine your sexuality now and as far back as you can remember. Get in touch with your conscience and try to understand what a tremendous impact your sexuality has on every aspect o your life. Once you understand the connection between your sexuality and your spirituality, your life will be transformed.**

Before Chris, I never saw myself as sexy and I have always been somewhat afraid of sex. I realise now that my poor body image and low self-esteem have never allowed me to feel sexy. Things are on the up now though, I can look at myself in the mirror and like myself a little more.

I am getting acquainted with the inner me. I quite like her! Chris and Lise have woken up my inner goddess, I do enjoy sex with Chris, I do feel great during and after! When I am in his arms I feel sensual and I am becoming more adventurous with sex, positions, naughty texts, lingerie ... during my lunch hour I now pay frequent visits to Ann Summers and fewer to Pret!

- **The next time you have intercourse, examine your feelings afterward. Did you accept if for what it was? Was it done out of love? Are your values preventing your from fully enjoying your relationship?**

I always have intercourse with love, we are in LOVE Lise ☺💣

Let's be honest now, I really don't have much to compare it to. It's not that I don't have sex experience, I just don't remember much of my experiences ...as always I blame the alcohol, but I do feel about sex with Brad Pitt, I mean Chris!

- **Repeat the following affirmation often and go on the next chapter.**

I AM A MANIFESTATION OF GOD ON EARTH, THEREFORE MY SEXUALITY IS ALSO A MANIFESTATION OF GOD. I USE MY SEXUALITY TO ELEVATE MY SPIRIT

Good night Mac!

x

OMG Mac . . . I don't know how to feel tonight ... unsettled, happy, anxious, scared, a little jealous? . . .

I managed to have a catch up with Mille and Jamie tonight. Millie managed to take herself away from Marco - they came back from Rome more loved up than ever - and Jamie was home, packing, for New York! And what catch up it was, it was an explosive one!

Mille got engaged on Sunday and she is moving in with Marco at the end of the week! Jamie has brought his trip to New York forward and is leaving tomorrow! WT F . . . ??

I am happy for Millie, she has finally got her over her commitment issues and I love Marco. He is the best thing that has ever happened to her! He truly loves her and brings out the best in her. But he is taking her away from me AND for good!

As for Jamie, he was supposed to leave at the end of this month, but has decided to allow himself some extra time in NYC to settle in. Honestly though, did he have to go so soon? Tomorrow? Apparently Virgin Atlantic had a mega sale on New York flights!

Don't worry Mac, I know what you are thinking. I won't have to move out and thankfully I won't have to find other flat mates! Millie said that for now she will not sell the flat. Did I have mention that this is her flat and I pay very little rent to her? 'I love you too much to leave you in the shit and I would like to have a Pied-à-Terre in East London, you know, should things not work out with Marco'. Bless her and her commitment issues! Jamie will also keep his room and pay his share of the rent. Phew! No need to move out, but I will be so lonely! Who knows, maybe if I tell Chris, he might want to move in with me?

I am happy for my friends, they have all changed so much, are moving on and I ... well, that feeling of loneliness is deepening in me! I know I have Chris, but I feel sort of stuck.

Chris makes me feel better, but I must confess ... I am so afraid of losing him! Last night I had a terrible nightmare, I dreamt that we had an argument and he said 'I can't do this anymore, I don't want to be with you anymore, I don't love you anymore!'. I have been in a funny mood all day... and the bombshells dropped on me this eve just amplified my anxiety.

Jamie did not want a proper send off, so we had a cheer with the champagne that was in the fridge, courtesy of Millie, who only drinks Champagne! I have been faking happiness all night, my jaw hurts from the pain of my fake smile.

I need to take my mind off things, I am going to work about chapter 13, 'Physical Essentials'. Thankfully work was very slow today and I managed to take a full lunch hour, read my chapter and did the exercises. There goes something positive for the day. Oh well along with seeing my love at work of course ☺. .. although ... my love must have been so busy today as he didn't even have the chance to reply to my e-mails. Or maybe he is dumping me? Oh my bloody anxiety starting ... bloody dream! I must learn to be cool. Chris is so right when he tells me to take a chill pill! Cool Kate, cool, calm and collected!

Let's move onto Lise.

Basically Lise says that we need to learn to pay attention, communicate with our physical body. Failure to do so will result in disease.

'There are six essential needs for the physical body. They are: breathing, ingestion, digestion, elimination, exploration and exercise.'

'**BREATHING** *is the body's most important physical need. If you stop breathing, even for a matter of seconds, the result is disastrous.*' I thought that food was the most important physical need!

Apparently if we breathe correctly, we only need to eat once a day! Tell that to those silly personal trainers, eat every 3 hours! Maybe that's how Jamie lost all of his weight? He is breathing more efficiently and eating once a day? Speaking of Jamie, he looked rather glorious last night, there is something about him these days, it must be his aura. – I know; I am so new age! Spiritual gypsy Kate! –

He is going to find a girlfriend in no time in NYC, his British accent will break many hearts, I know it!

'**INGESTION** *means the taking in of food and water into the body.*' Naturally the lack of will mean death, but apparently the quality is most important! It appears that the water we drink is nutritionally poor and she advises that we drink bottled water. But about the environment, I say? I drink plenty, water is not a problem and we are provided with bottled water at work, so tick for me!

She then went on to make an interesting point about eating meat. And got me a little confused. Lise asks to consider that *'when eating meat, the animal was frightened when it was slaughtered he was terrified by the smell of blood in the slaughter house and this fear produced a rush of adrenaline in its own tissue. This adrenaline stays in the body and becomes poison for the human who eats it.' 'Once you become more in tune with your body, your taste for meat and polluted water will diminish.*

Thanks a million! Now, what do I do? Chris tells me that it's most natural to eat animals, that human beings are at the top of the food chain and that we have always eaten meat. My mum, Lise and now newly vegan Jamie say that considering vegetarianism would be beneficial??? Oh what to do!??

Frankly, I don't necessarily enjoy eating meat or fish for that matter, but Chris gets a kick out of seeing me tucking into some meat! He looks like he is really proud of me!

'Listen carefully to your body. It knows what it needs and it is you best friend – treat it with love and respect. When you have a craving for something in particular, ask yourself if it is really something your body requires or if the craving is coming from some external influence.' That's for sure, before Chris I used to crave chocolate every day and I ate it every day, now, I don't crave it anymore. Love diet frees you of cravings!

*'Efficient **DIGESTION** is critical in maintaining good health, whether your body is fed food or new ideas. . . . Chew your food well, until it loses its flavour and becomes almost liquefied. This process aids digestion by giving the stomach less work to do… and the effort to swallow will be minimized. … by taking it a little easier on your stomach and your entire digestive system, you will leave longer and your quality of life will be much improved.'*

'**ELIMINATION** *is aided by good chewing and proper digestion. Fibre also plays a key role in efficient digestion, as it acts as a broom in cleaning out the intestinal tract .... Elimination is carried out, not only through the intestinal tract, but also through the kidneys and bladder and through the skin. (The skin is largest organ of elimination in the body). ... Many skin problems are a sign that the person is blocking his own personality. He controls himself, fearing the opinions or judgment of others. The message is 'Be yourself, let go, don't be afraid of what others might do or say. You have the right to be yourself'.*

I think Lise is so right on this skin thing. Look at Jamie, he had seriously bad skin, and look at him now! He has changed, he has obviously accepted himself and suddenly poof! Gone . . . Lise is a miracle worker, she is totally changing my life! I can now see and explain things I could not before!

'**EXPLORATION** *is a basic human need. This may come as a surprise to you, but one who does not utilize his senses becomes immobilized and his body stagnates until it becomes toxic and death is imminent'* Yuck! *'Human beings need to be active to keep the body functioning!'* I sure am! I am doing much more exercise and I am getting loads more action, if you know what I mean ;)! sex burns a lot of calories indeed!

'**EXERCISE** *is vital in keeping the body functioning on every level'.* Lise says that walking is the best form of exercise we can get. Wow, don't tell that to the fitness industry! Personal trainers would be out of business. I can't say that I enjoy exercise that much, running, well jogging in particular. But it's a great weight loss tool! Although Jamie did not agree with me the other night when I told I want to up the running, ok jogging to get down to a size 8. He was so sweet, he said that I am perfect the way I am and that exercise should do be something that I enjoy and not something I do to lose weight. Maybe he is right? After all, he did drop a lot of weight and did not do any running?? Honestly I am getting confused! Jamie does yoga and his body transformation is astonishing ... on the other hand, Chris is a gym bunny – and boy he looks great – he is down the gym every day, some days twice a day. He is perfect and he is great inspiration for me! Who is right? I want to be perfect for him, and I must get down to a size 8. He loves those women on Sports Illustrate and well, I am want to look like that!

'MENTAL EXPLORTION is also vital to the health of your physical body. If your actions, thoughts, words and feeling immobilize you and keep you from going forward in your life, you will experience problems in the legs arms, ears or nose ...EVERY ILLNESS IS A SIGNAL THAT YOU ARE THINKING SOMETHING THAT DOES NOT BENEFIT YOUR TRUE SELF'.

Our bodies are extraordinary! That's why I have decided that tomorrow I will do a full day of juicing. I want to detox and I have read somewhere that I can lose up to a kilo, <u>in one day</u>! How difficult can it be?

I better go get myself a snack before I move onto the exercises. Something healthy, a protein bar! Chris suggested I eat 2 a day as snacks and that my meals should be some white animal protein (chicken, turkey or fish), broccoli and a little brown rice. It 's not going to be that difficult seen that I now live by myself!

But I am going to juice tomorrow as I want to speed up the weight loss progress. I am still very sure he is soon going to invite me as his plus one at the wedding and I have to look slim for it! I will be representing my man!

CHAPTER 13 EXERCISES

- **Make a list of the six basic physical needs. Next to each one, make a note of the signals you have been able to recognize in your own body. It is your responsibility to decide to give your body what it needs. By taking responsibility for your own life, you will learn to please yourself and by listening to your body you will transform your life!**

This is a difficult one Mac? I am not sure???

BREATHING? I have never really paid any attention to my breathing? I thought it was an automatic thing? I recognize that when I run/jog I find it harder to breathe. But I don't think this is what Lise means. I will start paying more attention to it.

INGESTION. Nope, no signals either? As I have identified in the previous chapter I notice that when I am happy and excited – especially about seeing Chris – I don't feel like eating. As for the eating meat, for now I will carry on as I don't want to disappoint Chris! I should have also started to keep a food diary, but I don't have time Mac! Although, thanks for my boyfriend, I am becoming more aware of what I eat, when and the portions.

ELIMINATION. Probably I don't chew enough. I need to take my time over my food. I also read it in Grazia, 'if you want to lose weight, be mindful and chew your foods until they are liquid'. Noted! I wolfed down that chocolate protein bar. Was I mindful? Nope! Sorry! But I quite enjoyed it! I have even sent my boyfriend a text to tell him! I know, I keep repeating myself with the word boyfriend!

EXPLORATION. I am a little sedentary, my job requires me to sit for long hours and I probably do some exercise, like jogging and Pilates about twice a week, maybe 3 tops! Must do more! Maybe I should join the gym? I just find it so boring and intimidating though!

EXERCISE. As above!

MENTAL EXPLORATION. I am certainly more aware of my thoughts and the words I speak. These days I am most on the up, but I still notice thoughts and words of loneliness. I thought that once I had a boyfriend I would not feel that way. I think it is because I hate my job and my friends have all left. The exercises in this book are really helping me make sense of my life! Hopefully once I finish the book, I will have a clearer idea of what to do for a leaving and I will move in with Chris, fingers crossed! Then I will feel complete!

- **At this point, you have learned that it is imperative you remain alert to the needs of your physical body through your Superconscious mind. REMAIN ALERT!**

YES MADAM! I should make more of an effort!!!

- **Repeat this affirmation as often as you can think of it.**

I AM NOW DETERMINED TO RESEPCT THE NEEDS OF MY PHYSCIAL BODY AND REGAIN MY PHYSCIAL HEALTH

Wish me luck with the juicing tomorrow Mac

Kate x

Tuesday 26th May

Dear Mac

Boy oh Boy! That juicing is hardcore! It's now 6.30 pm and I have managed not to eat a thing, but I feel I am going mad! All I think about is food! Chris is totally supportive of me. He thinks it is great that I look after myself and that I want to slim down ☺ This is the e-mail he sent me: 'Keep strong sexy, I am so proud of you. It's good that you want better yourself, lose weight, get fit! I think you will look amazing as a size 8, just make sure you don't lose those big jugs of yours!'

He sooo sweet, I have got to stay strong

So far today I drank. 3 Naked Green Machines. They are yummy! And about 3 black coffees and 3 green teas. I need some caffeine to keep me going. Now I feel like I am climbing the walls, so hyped up! Fake energy for sure!

But Fear Not! My Love, My Saviour is coming after his gym session. There was no way I could go for a jog this evening, don't want to work out on an empty.

I told him that I won't be cooking for him, I don't think that I can be strong to cook and not eat. He said that it would have been the ultimate challenge for me, but he understands, so he will get a take away. How did I end up with such and understanding boyfriend? So to prove to him that I am worthy of him, I sent him a text telling him that I take on the challenge and will cook for him! I am crazy and in love woman!

Jamie left this morning, luckily we got to say good bye. We hugged and I could not hold the tears. I already miss him! It's such a shame that as boyfriends and girlfriends come into the picture we have to lose friends! Chris came into my life and Jamie and Millie left, hopefully not for good! It's amazing how life can change in the space of few weeks …it makes me feel very anxious.

Millie is upstairs packing, I better off helping her than analysing my life and I have to keep my mind off food!!

Self affirmation for me today, STAY STRONG KATE, YOU CAN DO IT, YOU ARE A SIZE 8!

Yay!

Laters Mac

Xxx

I am so upset and angry Mac …

Tonight Millie and Chris met for the first time and it did not go well ☹. Not well at all! I am disappointed and upset. Here is a little account … I must warn you Mac, there was a lot of alcohol and no food and emotions were running high!

M: Thank you so much Honey for helping out.

Me: you are welcome, it will give us a chance to catch up, I feel like I have not seen you in ages.

M: I know hon, I am sorry, life has been a little crazy. You know how intense Marco is. How are you? How are things for you? Here, have a glass of champagne.

Me: Thank you, well, where can I start ... I am in Love with the most gorgeous and amazing man in London and as you can see I lost a considerable amount of weight!

M: You look awesome Kate, very fit! Is it love that made you lose all this weight? You do look positively glowing! He must be a really good guy and he must treat you well, right?

Me: He has already told me that he Loves Me! Me, can you believe it?

M: Why not? You are amazing doll and anybody would be lucky to have you!

Me: you say that because you are my friend! But thank you. When he told me he loves me the first time my heart felt like it was going to explode. I am so happy, sometimes I cannot stop smiling, every time I see him I get fluttery butterflies in my stomach! There are so many of them that there is literally no space for food! Mind you there is always space for alcohol though!

M: You are funny

Me: He is so amazing, he is literally m everything! He helps me at work, with my fitness regime, he pushes me to do things I wouldn't normally do! And the sex ... well, it's amazing. I know I keep using that word, but it is by far the best adjective to describe him!

M: Aww Honey that's is so great. Everybody deserves to be in love and to enjoy new experiences

Me: and I now eat meat!

M: What? Why? You have been vegetarian since you were born. Your mum conceived you as a vegetarian. And I thought you did not believe in eating animals?

Me: I know, but Chris explained to me that eating meat is the most natural thing for humans. We are at the top of the food chain. And you know what Millie, I have realized that my belief of not eating meat came from my mum. She decided for me! I am my own woman now, a woman who is loved by an amazing man! A man who loves when I eat meat! And anyway, you eat meat so what is the problem?

M: Okaaayyyy . . . well whatever makes you happy Honey... . just as long as you are happy with your decisions . . .

Me: Chris helps me at work, with my exercise and diet. He is such a support! He always has my back!

M: WOW! I can't wait to meet him!

Me: I always felt that he was an unreachable dream! He is actually coming over in about an hour, after the gym! I am about to get his dinner ready.

To give you an example of how amazing he is. Today's fasting was really his suggestion, he thought it would be good for me as it would help shed the extra pounds and fast. And he sent me a very supportive e-mail this morning! He is such a sweetie!

M: Right ...- she said with a cynical tone and raised one of those perfectly shaped beautiful eye brows of hers to express her doubt. It made me feel a little uneasy and I gulped down more champagne.

Me: don't look at me like that, he is pushing me out of my comfort zone, he even asked me to cook for him tonight to prove to myself how strong I am!

M: That's fucking torture Honey, it's not support!

Me: I don't see it that way ... he wants me to push myself – my voice was shaking!

M: Ok don't get upset, let's agree to disagree

Me: yes, let's and if you don't mind, I am going to make some food for him now. Salmon, broccoli with brown rice. One of his favourites.

M: lovely, he is very healthy your Chris, isn't he?

Me: Wait till you see him!

~~~~~~

Mac, you would have been proud of me, I cooked and I didn't even try the food, not once. Once again, Chris has proved to be a star in my life. I rose to the challenge! And I am so proud of myself!!

I finally had a chance to introduce Chris to Millie, I think he must have been very tired as he barely said hello to her. No eye contact, nothing, very odd! Stubborn Millie did not get the hint that he was not in the mood for a chitchat and went on interrogating him about work, gym, home ... but my poor love was so tired and hungry that he did not even have the energy to speak to her. He mumbled a few words and tucked into his food. Poor lamb.

Thankfully Millie had dinner plans with colleagues and had to leave. I could sense she was a little irritated and I followed her to her bedroom, leaving Chris to catch up on the football

Me: Millie, are you ok?

M: I am sorry Kate, but he is a dick!

Me: Excuse me? You don't even know him

M: He has bad attitude! He wasn't even bothered to make conversation with me. Does he know I am one of your best friends?

Me: He does, but he is tired and hungry! The world does not revolve around you! Can you cut him some slack? – I was shaking with anger and disappointment. Not to mention that I was a little drunk and hungry!

M: Whatever, I don't want to get into a fight with you. First impression, not good. He is good looking, I can give you that. But his attitude stinks! Did you not notice that he didn't even thank you for making him dinner?

Me: I am sorry you feel that way. He is a good guy and he is just very tired and he was not expecting you to see! Maybe in his head he was expecting to just chill! Is Marco always perfect?

M: Marco is not perfect, but he always makes an effort with my friends, has Marco ever ignored you? He is always so kind and cordial toward you.

Me: Millie, he was tired and hungry. I will prove it to you. I will arrange a double date and you will get to meet charming, not tired Chris

M: Ok Honey, I love you and I want you to be happy. So go now, spend time with him. Take the bottle, you two can finish it. She gave me a hug.

Chris stayed a little longer, even though we barely talked, he seemed a little distant. I still loved spending time with him though. There is no need to always make conversation! He did not want to spend the night as he doesn't want us to go into work together. He thinks that if people knew it would cause problems for us. Again, what can I say, he is always so thoughtful! One thing is for sure though, I wish he had spent the night! One of the more reasons for hating work!

Good night Mac

K x

Wednesday 27th May

Hi Mac!

I am in a much better mood today; maybe it is because I lost a whole kilo yesterday! Whoop hoop! I am so happy right now! I have just tried those jeans I bought as motivational tool for my many diets, they are size 8 and although I cannot button them fully, I am almost there! I reckon a few more days of fasting and I am there! Sooo happy! 'Nothing feels as good as skinny feels' Kate Moss once said! She is absolutely right, I feel amazing when I fast. It's very hard though!

Work was boring as usual and Chris was as sweet as usual. He sent me this e-mail this morning:

'You are looking skinny, hot and glowing this morning, are you still fasting? Skinny suits you, you look like Jennifer Love Hewitt. Skinny with knock out boobs!

'Thank you my gorgeous man, I am loving my new figure, but I am not fasting today. I am going to keep it light, but I need some food. I will go back on the juicing tomorrow.

I was wondering if you would like to go on a double date with Millie and Marco on Sunday? I would love for my boyfriend and my best friend to get to know each other better.

He replied: 'Double dates are not my thing, but I will make an exception for you. On one condition . . .

Me: 'anything'

Chris: 'The internal position for account manager, can you get me an interview?'

Me: 'of course, consider it done! I will arrange both double date and interview now!'. I like that he is ambitious! He is really not qualified for the position, but I believe that he can do it. He achieves anything he puts his mind to.

And so I did both, Chris has interview next week and the double date is on Sunday we are going for brunch! Yay! Can't wait!!!!

And I have been very good with my food today, I only had soup for lunch, I am on a 'get skinny' roll! And ... red Chapter 14, 'Value Systems'.

I loved it, although a little hard to digest . . . Lise challenges me all the time with her concepts and philosophy and in this chapter she reminded me of my mum!

Here are some extracts from the chapter,

'Since the beginning of time mankind has been guided by its notion of right and wrong. Unfortunately, that notion varies from one individual to another and is determined by individual perception. What is determined to be "wrong" is usually based in fear. One person's interpretation of "wrong" behaviour, based on fear, can be interpreted as "right" by someone who is not afraid of t. The truth is, what is often perceived as "wrong" is merely part of the great Divine Plan and exists as a lesson pertaining to the evolution of mankind.'

Interesting concept Mac . . . There is no right and there is no wrong, everything is a lesson. Did I really get it right? Is it possible? Surely violence on children is not right!?? I am sure there are gray areas.

However, I think Millie could do with reading this. She was so upset that Chris asked me to cook for him, whilst fasting. She thought it was wrong of him, but I thought he was showing how much faith he has in me. He loves me and wants me to thrive!

There goes a lesson for Millie! She can be very judgmental! With her it's either her way or the high! But then again, here I am, judging her! She loves me and she looks out for me, she is very protective of me. Her judgment came from a place of love!

In any case, reading this chapter made me realize that I do live according to rigid ideas of what is right and what is wrong!

'Do you live your life organizing every hour of it based on your concept of right and wrong? How often do you prevent yourself from doing something that you would like to be doing because it wouldn't be right or because your concerned about what others would say about it?' YES! THIS IS SO ME! *'By refusing to do what we know inwardly we need to do, we become out of tune with ourselves. We become creatures of habit, accepting the external influence of right and wrong and structuring our lives around it.'*

Light bulb moment for me! This is exactly what I do! I am doing a job that I hate, but I keep doing it because "it is the right thing to do", "I am lucky to have a job"! At work I am constantly stressing because, let's be honest, I want people to like me, but nobody likes me! They think I am a bitch – apart from Chris of course! Who likes a Human Resources Manager? I HATE MY JOB!

Lise explains that ' *If you find that you are bothered by events and behaviours around you and that you react with guilt, fear, sadness, etc, it is because your mind is telling you it is "wrong". You are out of synch and out of alignment with your true self.' 'It is the Law of Divine Order that mankind live in peace and harmony. MANKIND ONLY EXPERIENCES DISCOMFORT WHEN HE LIVES CONTRARY TO NATRUAL LAW. Under the Law of Cause and Effect, there is no right or wrong – THERE ARE NO ERRORS – THERE ARE ONLY EXPERIENCES!'*

I GOTTA GET OUT OF MY JOB, IT'S NOT RIGHT FOR ME! I WANT A NEW LIFE

There, that's off my chest now!

This next paragraph brought tears to my eyes as it made me realize more stuff about me!

'Take a long, deep look at your own set of principles and values. Do they align with your goals? Do you believe them in your heart and do they bring you peace and happiness? The fact that you still feel a need to function according to outside rules and beliefs is an indication that the notion of right and wrong is still too strong in your life. This behaviour limits your growth and brings about continuous inner conflict. "I must not . . . should not…, it's just not right" is behaviour typical of those who cannot let themselves go. They are unable to free themselves of constraint and enjoy their inner child!

SADLY THIS IS ME! AND MORE SAD IS THAT I AM REALLY NOT QUIITE SURE WHAT MY PRINCPLES AND VALUES. I AM NOT SURE I HAVE EVER KNOWN, I DO LIVE ACCRODING TO WHAT IS "RIGHT" AND WHAT IS "WRONG"!

'Truth Is Relative to the perception of the individual'. If Only I knew my own truth . . .

'When your notion of right and wrong becomes too strong, you become rigid in your judgment and yourself and others. You lose the

*"MOMENT", the "NOW", by living in all "should have, could have",
critical, judgmental frame of mind.*

I can tick this box! The person I judge the most is myself! When I
describe myself as 'Gorilla with Cellulite', I am not exactly being
kind to myself . . . .. I am not exactly generating positive energy! To
create my own rules, to master my own life, I will need to learn to
Listen to My Body!

Can it be possible that the answers are in me? In my body? How
do I tap into them? I have only gotten accustomed to feeling a void
inside of me. A void which makes feel so restless that I need to fill
with food and alcohol!

*'The more you learn about mastering your own life, the fewer the events,
the less people or outside vibrations will have influence over you. You
may have experienced situations where, afterward you had said:' I don't
know what came over me- I just wasn't myself". A situation similar to
that happens to most of us at some point – it is not usual. Eventually,
however, your own mastery will give you the upper hand in such
situations and you will be able to eliminate them. DO NOT JUDGE
YOURSELF OR OTHERS – EVERY ONE OF US IS DOING OUT
BEST AT ANY GIVEN TIME.'*

My mum says this all the time! But until now I thought this was all
hippy dippy crap! How can you not judge violence and ill behaviour
of some people? Because according to spiritual principles we all
come into physical life to learn from our experiences! Trying not
to judge these spiritual principals really …. a challenge!

Hopefully the exercises will help me grasp this further. But before I move on, here is a tip from Lise, that I would like to share with you Mac.

'When you say: *"I have to"*, *you are clearly indicating that the notion of right or wrong has a great deal of importance to you'*. Lise suggest to replace "I have to" with "I choose to". It's more empowering and it does not turn us into victims. So from now on, I CHOOSE TO . . . ☺

Let's move onto the exercises:

- **Make a list of everything you consider right or wrong in life. Is your notion of right and wrong consistent with others? Do you assign the same values to yourself as you do others? Do you do unto others as you would have them do unto you? (Example: do you tell a cashier that she has given you too much change?)**

Violence, injustice, bullying, being nasty, judging is pretty much what is wrong in life! What is right is to be a good person, help others, be kind, pay compliments and be respectful of others. Oh, let's us not forget, 'thank you', something that my boss often forgets to say!

Do I assign the same value to myself as I do others? No Lise, NO! I judge myself, I criticize myself, I don't help myself, I am not kind to myself! But I would say that this is because I am a bit of a perfectionist, I want to improve myself! If I am not strict with myself, how will I ever improve?

I always treat others very well, I never contradict people, I am easy going, I can see their point of view, and frankly I hate conflict! Do others treat me the same way? HELL no! I feel constantly judged, criticized and when I was younger I was bullied because my mum turned me into a weirdo! And I quite resent her for it!

Basically I do not treat myself well and others either ignore me or criticize me. Millie and Jamie are the only ones who truly love me and accept me for who I am. Mama and Papa' say I am their special girl, but I don't think they give a shit! But I am used to it, I have learnt to accept them for who they are.

-   **Go over the list and determine whether the things on your list are definitely right or wrong, or are they 'sometimes right, sometimes wrong', depending on the circumstance, the people involved, etc. In doing so, understand that there is no absolute right or wrong – nothing that applies to everyone, in every situation.**

Well Lise, I know according to your philosophy there is no right or wrong as it is all a learning process. But I am not there yet. It's a difficult concept to accept. How can violence be right too? I am not saying that Lise is wrong, I am just saying that I am having a hard time digesting this information, but in time I might get there.

-   **Make a second list of your habits**

I am in the habit of pleasing people, I find it hard to say no, I don't like people getting upset with me. I put myself down, I don't take compliments (because I think that people must have ulterior motives), I am hard on myself, but that's because I have high standards. I am the queen of excuses! ☺

I am very regimented in my eating habits (I have allotted times), I count calories, I always have my coffee black and in the same coffee shop, I always listen to music on my way into work, I keep a journal at the end of each day, Yes….I see where this is going, I am creature of habits! Must be spontaneous and listen to my body!!!

- **Over the next 3 days, change at least one habit consciously you must replace it with a beneficial one of your own choosing. Understand that many of your non-beneficial habits were developed through outside influences – your surroundings, your education, even decisions you made as a young child. You will recognize a positive habit – it vitalizes, invigorates and motivates you – it may even inspire you! IMPORTANT * REMEMBER THAT YOUR HABITS SHOULD BE THE RESULT OF A CONSCIOUS CHOICE!**

I can think one I can do from tomorrow, I am going to stop to say 'Yes' when I don't mean it. I will take that power!

- **Repeat this affirmation:**

I AM AWARE OF ALL MY HABITS SO AS TO REALZIE WHICH ARE OF BENEFIIT TO ME IN MY DEVELOPMENT AND ARE CONTRIBUTNG TO MY HARMONY. I ACCEPT THAT LIFE IS A CHOICE I HAVE MADE.

Feeling deflated! it is quite clear to me that I need to do some serious work on myself! Good night Mac!

K x

Hi Mac

A pretty uneventful today and I cannot help being a little worried about Chris, he did not come into work today and I have not heard from him? I texted and called him, but have not heard back.

Maybe he is ill? Or just plain hangover. Know he went out with the boys last night and maybe today he is suffering for it? Yet it is odd that he would not get in touch with me? I just hope he has not ended up in hospital!

Today I feel pretty down, partly because I have not heard from my love and partly because I just do! I think it is PMS. On top of that I feel lonely. Millie has pretty much moved out, sooner than expected! And I got an e-mail from Jamie, who I miss loads!

This is his e-mail

'Hello my lovely Kate,

How are things with you? I hope that you are still high on love and are enjoying the beginning of summer in London.

I have arrived in NYC and although it has been a few days, I am in love with it already! It has amazing vibes, my flat (well Millie's and BTW how rich is she!??) is just like the ones you see in the movies! My 2 flat mates, Sylvia and Tom, seem to be pretty cool too. They are throwing me a welcome party this Friday and I expect to meet loads of new people! I tell you what, my English accent is proving to be very popular with the ladies. I am getting loads of attention, which is so new to me! Who would have thought that a geek like me would get so much attention and from some very attractive girls!

I wish you were here, I know for a fact that you would love it here! My course starts in a couple of weeks, and so I am planning to explore NYC and of course carry on my yoga practice. I really suggest you try it out, yoga has changed my life!

Has Millie moved out yet? I will get in touch with her at some point, but I just wanted to check in with you and check that all is well. You seemed a little down when I left. I hope Chris is treating you well, because if he doesn't I might just have to come and get you!

Stay beautiful and happy Kate

Love

Jamie x'

Nice ha Mac!? Although I am very happy for him, I can't help feeling a little jealous. He seems to be having a fab time out there, and I am here... he seems to be meeting all these new people ... I have no friends... ... and who are these attractive girls???

I am glad that all is well with him though and before I reply to him I will go check out the yoga class. Jamie knows me well, if he suggests it, I am sure I will enjoy. Actually let me google it now, I have nothing better to do tonight, maybe I can go tonight? Or maybe I shouldn't, just in case Chris needs me?

Found it, there is a class on tomorrow, it's on at 5.30, I will be done by 7. If Chris wants to do something I can catch up with him then.

I am feeling blah at the moment, I am not sure what triggered it? I don't fancy reading my book, I am just going to catch up with my vampire series, down some dark chocolate and wash it off with Pinot Grigio. Yes I do ...feel very sorry for myself. It must be PMS, it is such a nuisance. I will be fine tomorrow....but I am still wondering about Chris!

Laters Mac

Kx

Friday 29th May

Hi Mac!

Much better day today. I finally heard from Chris! He got food poisoning and his phone run out of power, that's why he did not get back to me. Just as well that he goes out with the HR manager, I have covered for him yesterday.

He didn't come into work today as he was still feeling under the weather and most likely I won't see him tonight. I just hope he is well for our double brunch date on Sunday! And I am hoping to have him all to myself on Monday! It's bank holiday weekend and I really want to spend some quality time with him! I miss him so much when he is not with him, I cannot stop thinking about him!

Work was ok, same old same . . .not worth talking about it. I stick with it for now as I am not sure what else I should be doing with my life. And I remember Lise's words, I choose to go to work ☺

I went to my first yoga class and although it was hard I enjoyed it! I feel positively knackered, but chilled and uplifted. Emma, the skinny with amazing abs teacher, got us in all these contortionist positions. I found them extremely challenging but beautiful. And then we chanted OM…. What on earth is OM?? Needless to say that I did not really follow the chant or meditate for that matter. But it was fun looking around and seeing how into it the other students were! Is yoga a cult? I will e-mail Jamie now.

'Hi Jamie

How are you? It is great to hear from you. I am so happy that you are already having such an amazing time in NYC! And what about all those amazing girls? The Americans love an English accent and let's face it, you are looking pretty good lately! All that yoga and vegan food is paying off ☺

Speaking of which, you will be proud of me, I did my first ever yoga class this evening. I loved it, you are right. It was a brand new experience for me. Emma, the teacher, was very cool, and although she put us into this rather odd poses, she was rocking some decent music! And at the end she got us to chant OM… what is that? I felt a little stupid sitting there with crossed legs, eyes shut, chanting. Well I didn't really manage to do it. It just felt a little odd!! The others were so into it, a bit cultish, I thought?

Despite it all, I will definitely go back, thank you for the tip!

As for my life here in London, well I can't say that it is as exciting as yours. Apart for my relationship, which is going really well, I feel quite empty and lonely! Maybe it's because the flat feels cold and empty without you and Millie.

Millie has moved in with Marco and she sounds really happy. We are going to have a double date on Sunday and really hope that things go better than the first time Chris and Millie met. Let's say he did not make a good first impression. She can be very judgmental, you know her, she has a strong personality. And before you say anything, I know, she has my best interest at heart. She comes from a place of love, and I have forgiven her.

Chris and I are doing well, I have not seen much of him this week as he is not well, but our love is growing stronger and I am hoping that he will invite me as his plus one to his best friend's wedding at the end of June.

Nobody really knows about us, apart from you and Millie. He is very reserved and does not like to talk about his personal life. And it is best that people at work don't know. We don't want to start some silly gossip.

Not much else is going on with me, I am hating my job more and more and as much as I want to get out of it, I just don't seem to understand what I want to do with my life. Sometimes I wonder who I am and I question all that I have done in my life up to now.

I am sorry Jamie, I am feeling a little down, women's things ... all is fine really, I just miss you and Millie. I need time to adjust. I wish I was in NYC with you, maybe I will come and visit soon. I need to save some money first. How come I am always skint?

I am going to go now, have a fab party and be good

Love

Kate x'

That's sent, let's see if he can shed some mystery on the OM!

The yoga class has inspired me to read Chapter 15 now, The Ego. I didn't get the chance at work today. I will come back to you Mac as soon as I am done.

… ….

Me again… Difficult chapter! I had hoped it would help me to figure out a few things about myself, but now I feel even more confused about who I am. Lise was right when she said that this process would be a very painful one!

The Ego seems to be a monster that resides in us and that must be tamed and mastered.

'"Ego", or false pride, is an uncomfortable subject for most people to discuss. All of these stem from fear – and so we are face to face with fear that we have tried our whole lives to cover up with ego. Although aware of our Divine Perfection subconsciously, we have yet to understand the need to surrender to its simplicity and guidance. We still need to "control". I have yet to meet a person who has completely mastered the ego, although every religion honours someone who has.'

Yeah, no, I can't think of anyone who has mastered the ego either. I think even my mum is still working on it. As much as I think of her as mother Teresa, I know she sometimes tries to control my father. She is a bit of a control freak, my Mum and my dad is the total opposite. I remember when I was little, she used to yell at him because he was, still is messy! They screamed for 5 minutes and then she would back off and she would say "I am sorry, my ego got the best of me", my dad would reply "I don't understand you, you read all of these books and you still have not learnt to apply them!", "It's a working in progress Honey, it takes constant effort and work to change your thought process". It did not make sense then, but I get it now.

'Those with strong egos are easily identified – they continually seek to be "right", blaming, criticizing and judging others, trying to change them to feel superior.' Is that what Millie, Jamie and I do when we gossip? We criticize? We let our egos get the best of us? But I don't understand, it is fun, that's what keeps us close, that's what makes us click. What would we talk about if we did not gossip a little?

'Power over others, which is only an illusion, gives them the strength that they are lacking inwardly. The more egotistical a person seems outwardly, the more fear he is dealing with inside'. Mmmm, My BOSS IN ONE!

'Mankind's ego is its greatest downfall – it is the root cause of rivalries between individuals and nations, wars, intrigue and hatred. It breeds a shallow, empty power but hardens the heart and prevents love. Ego –driven people deem themselves "winners", but are, in truth, the real losers'. So true! True to say that the ego is the root of all evil. Maybe that's what the devil is, our ego!

'By allowing your ego to overtake you, you stand to lose many things. The repercussions in your relationships, your health and your happiness are severe. You will perceive life as a constant "fight", an uphill battle. Is it worth it?'

No, that's why I don't believe in fighting, but ...according to Lise, people with big egos are not just those who think they are always right and want to win all the time. No they are also those who appear to be humble! *'The opposite of ego is humility. Be careful, though, many people who consider themselves humble are actually exhibiting a false humility that masks fear and weakness causing them to give up easily. Give those people some power and a false pride rapidly emerges, replacing their 'humility'. Those who cannot accept compliments, who put themselves down in terms of their talents and abilities, are acting from false humility, which is another form of ego.'*

Question. Has Lise written this book for me?

'The true self is fully aware of its talents and abilities and it neither needs to hide them nor to blatantly expose them. It accepts them and nurtures them; it also feels no pride in them and not guilt for having them.' I guess Millie is very much like that. She is such a confident woman, she is an amazing lawyer, but she never shows off!

'If you must compare yourself with someone else whom you feel is superior to you in any way, do so by understanding that God's presence is in all of us and that person is expressing his God-self more effectively than you. You will understand that there is always much to be learned from other.'

'Ego resists all inner transformation and blinds you from seeing God in everything and everyone. It represses feelings and emotions and denies relationship with the true self. It will discourage you from self-improvement and will not allow you to forgive, lest you are perceived as "admitting you were wrong"

I know what you are thinking now, because I was thinking it too. What is the purpose of this ego? Was the ego also a creation of the Divine?

And naturally Lise answered that too. '*The purpose of the existence of the ego is to challenge you to overcome its illusion. When you are overwhelmed with ego, you are no longer yourself. The ego is the thorn that constantly irritates and keeps you aware that there is still more growing to do – as long as you continue to feel the thorn, you will be aware of the need to move away from it. Acknowledge it – give it a name if you wish. Whenever you are aware of its irritating presence, tell it that you no longer have any need for it. By doing so, you will have great impact on its disappearance and will no longer be under its influence*'

It doesn't make much sense to me. I mean … we were perfect then we are given the ego to challenge our illusions so that we become perfect? I don't know I must be thick!

'*Keep in mind that your ego is stubborn and will do whatever it takes in order to survive. It doesn't like to be mastered, as it perceives itself as the master. It will torment and attack you once you decide to do without it, especially the first few weeks following your decision to do so. In my own experience, it takes approximately three weeks for the ego's resistance to subside and for things to get easier*'

It's like exorcising a demon! Let's hope it won't be as dramatic and ugly as the Exorcist. Can you imagine my head spinning around and vomiting green?!

Exercises to help exorcise the ego!

>>Make a list of the people you have come into contact with over the past three days. You may have met with them, spoken with them, or merely thought of them.

Chris, Mum, Jamie, Stephanie, Vicky, my Boss, Millie, Marco

>> *Be totally honest with yourself. No one else will see what you*
are writing. If you like, you can burn the paper when you are done.
With each contact, ask yourself whether your ego got the better
of you – did you intellectual pride tell you " I knew best" or your
spiritual pride tell you " I am better"?

Sadly Lise, and this is the honest truth, I never think that I am
better than anybody else. Quite the contrary in fact! Compared
to these people, Chris, Mum, Jamie, Stephanie, Vicky, my Boss,
Millie, Marco, I feel like a total fraud and a bit fat loser. Is that
intellectual ego? More like battered ego!

Chris is absolutely perfect! Confident, handsome and intelligent!

Mum is a lousy mum, but she is also a confident, beautiful, kind,
intelligent woman. She is unapologetic for who she is!

Jamie is blossoming by the minute, he is like he has shed the negative
skin and becoming this beautiful, confident, creative, adventurous,
stylish, amazing young man, and I really miss him

Vicky, although she is a bit on a chubby size is super sweet, very
good at her job and she is married with 2 children.

My boss, well, he is rich and a dick!

Millie is perfect, beautiful, smart, wealthy and has an amazing
fiancé'.

Marco, is Mr Perfect. Millie and Marco are like Barbie and Big Jim!

Stephanie, you might ask, I don't even want to go there. She is all
I want to be! But she does not have my man! Chris! I still leave in

constant fear to lose Chris; I still have these nightmares that wake me up in the middle of the night in a pool of sweat! He cheats on me, he is mean to me, he pretends not to know me! I guess these are my own insecurities come through my subconscious!

>> *The point of this exercise is not to stir up guilt, but to raise your consciousness and clarify your position in respect to your ego. What did these responses, and your overall attitude, cost you in terms of inner peace, your social life, happiness and attitude toward others? Are you prepared to continue paying the price?*

Overall, it is clear that I think of myself as a big fat Loser! I don't know where these feelings are coming from. I thought that once I had Chris, once he had told that he loves, once I dropped a dress size and some more, I would feel better about myself? But the more I look at myself, deep down, the more I am honest with myself, and the less I see the light! What am I doing wrong? No, I am not prepared to continue to pay the price!

>>*Confront your ego directly and observe the changes in our life. They will be dramatic.*

>> *Take each incident on your list, one at a time, and discuss it openly with the person involved. Ask for forgiveness, if you need to, and tell them you realize it was your ego talking and not your heart. Admit, simply, that you are WORK IN PROGREASS and ask for their patience. That beautiful act of love will have tremendous significance in your growth . . . and theirs*

The only person I need to forgive is myself really. All the others are fine as they are. There is something wrong with me for sure! I will pay attention to my thoughts more and will work on seeing the good in me. But it won't be easy, I know it!

>> Here is your affirmation. Repeat it as often as you can:

I ACCEPT MYSELF AS I AM, EACH DAY LEARNING TO MASTER MY EGO BY SEEING AND FEELING GOD IN EVERYONE AND EVERYTHING AROUND ME.

Tougher than I thought Mac, but 'no pain no gain' as they say.

I really hope I get a good night sleep tonight

Good night

K x

Saturday 30th May

Hi Mac

Awful night sleep, I think that chapter has stirred up lots of feelings, I could not sleep. I ended up watching tv all night! There are so many wonderful tv series on Netflix ... They are like cherries, once you start, you can't stop!

But, and there is a but! Things are looking up and got a text from Chris this morning. "Hi sexy, I missed you last night, fancy a night in tonight? We can watch a movie and then go to your brunch thing together in the morning? x"

I feel better, but I still have this cloud of gray lurking around me, my period must be coming soon!

Anyway, better have a shower now, go for a run, shower again and do some food shopping. I feel in the mood for baking tonight, baking always calms me down! Maybe I will also check the shops for something new to wear for tonight. These days my closet seems to be empty! I don't know, I never seem to have anything to wear! I don't like anything I own and anyway … I need a new wardrobe, most of my stuff is too large! Which is fab!

Kx

I am so upset! It's 9.30 and no Chris. He just texted me 'I won't make it, something has come up. I will tell you tomorrow. I swing by your place at 10.30 x'

Lately I am seeing less and less of Chris, apparently his flat mate, best friend and groom to be is having cold feet about the wedding! And Chris is helping him out. It's nice that he wants to help him, but I feel neglected.

I was having a good day, did a 40 min jog along the Themes, soaked up the warm rays of this beautiful spring. Went to the health food shop up the road and bought the ingredients for the cake. I love buying from health food shops, but I always end up spending loads! Health costs, but you can't put a price on health! That's my excuse anyhow!

Then went to Urban Outfitters, got myself a fabulous pair of black leggings, a white long shirt, which I had planned to unbutton all the way down my cleavage (for Chris' benefit!), an deep orange jacket to go over it and a Vivienne Westwood bag - she is my mum's and mine! Favourite designer. This we have in common!- and some accessories. Ready to go, but where?? Well I can wear it tomorrow at brunch.

I love shopping, but lately retail therapy is no longer making me feel as great as it did... mmm, I am really not sure what is going on! PMS, that my excuse!

Got home, baked a carrot cake and really enjoyed myself, for me the kitchen provides meditations, it calms me down, it makes me feel happy. But I do try my food and a lot and then I feel guilty, I am so worried about getting fat. It's safe to say that my relationship with food is most certainly not a healthy one. Yes, there goes a surprise, not! Honestly what's wrong with me. I feel so down on myself.

But the cake is good, I have a slice laying just next to you Mac, it's delicious. I think I already had about half of it! Yes it is PMS!

I was all done by 5.30, I am very organized! Whilst waiting for Chris to come around I even read chapter 16 **'False Masters'.**

Much lighter than the previous chapter, but a good reminder on how to use my thinking in a more positive way.

'Firstly you must understand fully that there is only ONE TRUE MASTER, and that is your inner God – your God – self. Every human being has his own, individual mater within.'

This concept is very refreshing and enlightening, but I am still struggling with it.

The definition of master is *'"One with control of authority over another". Many people find that their lives are ruled, or run, by others (i.e. spouse, children, parents, authority figures, etc), a situation that is the result of fear.'*

'When you fear someone else, you are allowing him to become your master ... and you are no longer your own master. He will manipulate you constantly, as he knows exactly what triggers a reaction in you. Being in a reactive state is very draining on your energy and creates a choric emotional state that is detrimental to your physical, mental, and spiritual health'

Other False Masters are: *'**The News and weather reports; Power and recognition** : Doing something for the purpose of gaining recognition and /or power indicates that you are a slave to outside influence and not in control of your inner self. You are out of touch with your God-self and your true nature; **Material Possessions:** It is normal and healthy to want to be surrounded by beautiful things. Our environment is important to us. What is not beneficial, though, is to let material possessions rule your life. They are there to embellish your life, not to govern it.'*

Mum always says that material possessions don't bring you happiness. I am starting to think that she is right. Look Mac, I bought myself a whole outfit and a bag today and do I feel happier than I did yesterday? NOOOOO!

Retail therapy is a false therapy, I say!

*'**Astrology** can also become a false master, if used to guide your every direction.'* I would not say that my life is ruled by astrology, but truth be said, I read, daily, what my star sign has to look forward to.

And I always ask boys what theirs star sign is. Being a Gemini, my most compatible sign is Aquarius. But Chris is a Leo, astrologically speaking, it's not the best match! But look at us, we have fallen in love, so there you have it another false master!

'Clairvoyants and Mediums'. I personally think they are bunch of charlatans! But some people swear by them! *'Psychics, also known as "sensitive", or" channels", pick up on the vibrations of your subtle body. They are in tune with your current state of mind and current state of affairs as they relate to your vibration. They are able to tell you what will happen if you remain on the path you are on.* **As the future is entirely dependent on the choices you make right now.**

Ergo my future is dependent on the choices I am making right now! The 'Now' shapes the future! Need to make a note of this. Actually I want to share this with Jamie, who has not yet got back to me about the OM! And …come to think of it, Jamie is an Aquarius, it might explain why we get on so well!

'Hi J

How are you? How is NYC? Meeting fun people?

I miss you and Millie loads, it is hard to live in our beautiful 3 bedroom flat all by myself. I feel terribly lonely. But I am happy for you guys!

I am reading this self-help book, I told you about, and came across this sentence and wanted to share it with you

'The future is entirely dependent on the choices you make right now'

I am still not entirely sure what my choices are, lately I have been a little down and I don't know if it because my best friends are away, or because I hate my job, or both? I have lost a lot of weight, I have this wonderful boyfriend, he is truly is all I wanted (I thought), but I just don't feel as though I am in love with life. I have good days and bad ones and when I don't hear from him, I get so down in the dumps! I can't seem to be able to stop myself from being negative and unhappy about my life. I honestly do not know how to make myself happy. The book said that our thoughts and actions shape our lives, but as much as I try to stay positive, I just don't seem to get there.

Any suggestions? I admire you so much. You are so brave for having taken charge of your life and you now live your dreams! And don't tell me that I can do it, because I don't know what my dreams are!

Anyway, I don't want to bore you with my victim talk, I must sound so winy!

Hopefully tomorrow will be a better day for me. Chris and I are going to have a double date with Millie and Marco! Fingers crossed that Millie is in a good mood!

You have a wonderful weekend my friend and don't forget about the OM thing, what is that? I know I can google it, but I will understand it better if it comes from you ;)

I miss you

Kate x'

I feel better for sharing my feeling with Jamie, I don't feel like I can do the same with Chris. And lately he has been very distant. Mind you, he has been busy and I can be a bit neurotic. Kate be cool! Maybe I ought to try some camomile tea? I do drink too much coffee and I notice that it does not help my anxiety!

Let's carry on with chapter 16.

*'**Organised Religions**. Religions were organized centuries ago to establish a framework of behaviours for cultures that were not conscious enough to guide themselves. As with everything, there are positive and negative aspects to any religion that has developed for such purposes. Many of the religions, because they are created by human beings, are designed to control their follower by instilling fear in them. This is a terrible abuse of power and does not result in the balanced, harmonious existence that you desire. God is love – the concept of fear is manmade. ... Once you become more in tune with your inner knowing, you will understand what you need and will gravitate to a religion that is comfortable and beneficial to you.'*

I agree with Lise, I am not religious at all, I was raised believing that we are all 'extensions of God'. Whatever that means, I quote my mother!

My parents have taught me to be respectful of other people's beliefs and thus I don't really have an opinion on religions. For sure, I do not believe in killing in the name of God, no God would excuse killing! Me thinks!

*'**Doctors** sometimes fall into the 'false master' category. Once you learn to trust your inner master, you will find you have no need to continually consult your physician before making many of the decisions in your life.'*

I hardly see my doctor, I signed up for the hell of it, but I have only seen him twice in 8 years! I am generally healthy and don't believe in doctors and I was brought up that way.

Other false masters are:

Illness, Fashion, Work (yes most definitely my master! More like my tyrant!), Superstition, Ego, fear and Guilt (we have established that is most definitely my case in the previous chapter! Working on it though!) and Money.

Let's face it, isn't Money everybody's master? Who does not want more money??

However Lise gives some interesting concepts around the subject of money:

'Like all false masters, the preoccupation with money and the resulting control it has over a person's life, stems from insecurity and fear of being without. Ask yourself if your bank account determines most of your daily decisions. Is it limiting you in any way from getting what you want?' Yes Lise! I am in a job I ate because it pays the bills!

'It's time to adjust your attitude about money, so that you fully understand that it is energy to be tapped at will' Wow, right? Tell me more? ....

'Just like electricity, water and wind, money is a form that exists in abundance. Like all energies, it has power and is there for the taking. Accumulating it out of fear of not having enough, and hanging on to it, are indications of lack of faith or confidence in Divine Law'. Is she for real?

'*Compare money to sunshine. Whether there are 3 or 300 people sunbathing on a beach will have no bearing on the amount of sunlight being generated'.* Good analogy! '*It is very important for you to understand that money is energy – the more you allow it to circulate, the more it will flow into your life, gain power, momentum and multiply. . . . Letting go of financial insecurity can be a long process if you fail to understand its energy. Take a look back in your life. If there was something you desired a great deal, did you not find the money to buy it somehow? Did you suffer terribly having channelled that money into something you really wanted? I would venture a guess that you bought it and that it brought joy to you, enhancing your life and feeding your energy. YOU ARE WORTH IT!'*

So true, last year Jamie, Millie and I went on holiday to Ibiza. I couldn't exactly afford it, Millie and Jamie make considerably more money than me and have expensive taste. I struggle to keep up with them, financially that it is! I booked in on my credit card confident that I would pay it off eventually. A week later my dad surprised me with a cheque of £1K for my birthday! Daddy is very generous! He always helps me out with money!

We had an amazing holiday! Thankfully we were drunk pretty much all week long so I did not worry so much about what I looked like in a bikini! I don't want to think about it, I was size 16 last summer, I disgust myself!

'*The image you have yourself – your sense of SELF-WORTH is determined by you and you alone. Others mirror whatever opinion you have of yourself. If you prefer to keep money in case of bad luck, you will attract bad luck. If you prefer, instead, to honour yourself by taking a vacation*'– that's what I did ☺ - '*you will have appreciated what money can really do for your inner self. You will always manage, somehow, to make ends meet.*

Fair enough, enough said … I am going to fish this cake now and then watch some TV

Hasta luego, ciao, au revoir Mac!

Sunday 31st May

Dear Mac

What a miserable day for me! Another bloody one for me! Bruch with Millie and Marco was a total fiasco! Chris did not show up. He texted me this morning to tell me that he was not feeling well. I am so disappointed and I can't help worrying about this relationship. Things have been a little strained, it feels like he has been avoiding me. Maybe it's just me, I have to learn to chill and be cool!

Brunch with Mille and Marco was nice though, although I think Millie is not all fond of Chris. And I can't totally blame her!

Millie: K, your birthday is next Saturday, any plans? Shall we do something? I am sorry I have left it to the last minute; I have been so busy with everything!

Me: I know Honey and please do not worry about it. I honestly have no idea, I would love to spend some quality time with my friends and maybe boyfriend! But he has also been so busy lately and it all has taken its toll on his health! Poor lamb!

Millie: I am sorry to hear, he is not well today then? We were really looking forward to meeting him. What a shame, hopefully next time? It'd be nice for us to get to know him. Are things going well with you two? Are you still loved up!? Is he treating you well?

Is this what she is like at work? She can sure put an act on. I know she hates him, but she is showing a very diplomatic side!

Me: Oh yeah sure! -

I dropped my gaze as I know that she can read me well and she knows something is up

Millie: "You don't sound so sure, you know you can always talk to me. You can be honest with me and Marco, of course! (She gave Marco the sweetest kiss on the cheek. She is so vulnerable and sweet when she is with him. He truly brings out the best in her.

Me: I know Honey, thank you, but really, all is fine. You two just looks so sweet! How are the wedding preparations going?

Millie: You always do this Kate, change the subject! I do hope that one day will learn to let other people in, especially the ones that love you!

How can I Mac? How can I break down the walls? If I open up to Chris he will see who I really am, a weak, pathetic gorilla with cellulite! But I have been try to change for him, so Why is he so distant? Is he starting to see my true colours?

Mille and Marco told me all about their wedding plans and Millie asked me to be her maid of honour. Naturally I have accepted, she is my best friend and I am so happy she has found such a wonderful man. The wedding will be next year in September and she would like to use my parent's finca in Ibiza. She has already been in touch with my mum and she even asked her to be their minister. Fuck is there anything that my mum doesn't do? Oh yeah, she doesn't do motherhood!

When I got home, I checked my phone countless times . . . no messages. So I decided to get brave and show Chris my caring side and sent him a text. "I hope you are feeling better and hope to see you tomorrow in full health. I miss you so much, Kate x". His reply "Much better thank you, I am going to stay low tomorrow, but I will see you on Tuesday x". Nice text reply right? He put a X in the end, he must still have feelings for me! And let's face it Mac, men are not very good with words, they are very monosyllabic!

I'm off to bed now, I am so drained! It's been a very emotionally charged and tiring day. But I have a feeling that next week is going to be amazing! It's my birthday week and all I want to do is to spend time with my love!

Sweet dreams

Kate x

Monday 1st June

I am sorry Mac; I am not going to write anything ... just too depressed! It's bank holiday Monday and I am all alone in this big flat ... too depressed to do exercise, read, look after myself! It's 5.30 and I am still in my PJs ... so I am going to carry on with my pity party, numb myself out with TV, Ice Cream and Pinot! My new best friends!

Tomorrow will be a better day; it can only go up from here!

Night Mac x

Tuesday 2nd June

Hello Mac!

A positive day at long last! Sweet, sweet day indeed! Chris was back in the office, in splendid form and bombarded me with loads of flirty e-mails! He is coming to visit tonight after the gym! I am so happy, I cannot wait!

I have been such a silly girl! Paranoia, paranoia, I really ought to learn to be COOL!

There is one thing that today got on my nerves though, but I ignored it, because I am working on being cool! I was in the office kitchen this morning drinking having a catch up with Vicky, when Stephanie walked in and asked me how my weekend was. Very odd, she generally ignores me. Then she gave me one of those toe to head looks, she judges me? What a cow! I don't get why she dislikes me so much, I am nothing but nice to her!

Nonetheless, work was fine; I was in such a good mood! I also managed to get to the gym during my lunch break!

And I have also been super organized, on my way home I bought food shopping for tonight. I'm going to make Chris his favourite meal, Steak and Chips! I cleaned the flat and read chapter 17, 'Mental Essentials'. Short chapter, but as always insightful. Here is a little account.

'There are many fundamental needs of the mental body, a few of which I will discuss in this chapter. Failure to meet any of one of these needs will have a negative impact on your physical, mental, emotional and, especially, your spiritual life.

TRUTH is the most important need. It is the key to freedom, uplifting your higher body and expanding your vibration. To be "true" means that what you think, say and do are the same thing. When your words and actions do not coincide with your thoughts, you are out of alignment and your inner balance will be off. If someone asks you your opinion, you owe it to yourself to be truthful, for the sake of your own alignment, if nothing else.'

My question here is, 'Is truth always the best policy though?' I get what Lise is saying, but the truth can also hurt people's feelings and surely that's not nice and does not make anyone feel good, right??? Can I really tell Vicky (my assistant) that she would look much prettier if lost a few pounds? It would hurt her too much, she is very sensitive! And she has had 2 children, I hear that baby fat is very stubborn to shift!

'JUSTICE is an element of the truth. Note the discomfort that an act of injustice against you, or against anyone else causes you…. Your Superconscious mind, your soul, needs to be nurtured and kept whole. Any behaviour or attitude that is contrary to that wholeness is unhealthy. The body provides signals to the person who is not true or unjust to himself, by affecting the throat region and/or respiratory

system.' Funny that she mentions that, I always have to wear a scarf around my neck as I am prone to sore throats!

'INDIVIDUALITY, as defined by Webster, is "the aggregate of characteristics that distinguishes one person from others" You are unique and must respect and express that uniqueness to be true to yourself.' Yes true, if only I managed to figure out who I am! What makes me unique?? *'Stop concerning yourself with the opinion others have of you, or with their expectations of you. - BE YOURSELF'.*

I always act nice and polite because let's face it I don't like confrontation. Yet despite being nice and cordial I still have haters in the office. Look how Stephanie treated me today!

'RESPECT of ourselves and others is vital to our mental health and balance. It is terribly frustrating to have to respect someone of authority (i.e.: police, teachers, employers, parents etc.) when the respect is not mutual. A position of authority does not give one a license to disrespect and abuse others. No one is superior in any way on a soul level.' Maybe I should copy/paste this paragraph and e-mail it to my boss. He is such an ass! "Kate, your e-mails are always so vague, it is a though you have not got a back bone! Grow a pair old girl!" I know he is old school, but must he be so rude to me?

Lise finishes this paragraph with a mind boggling sentence, *'If others do not respect you, remember that they are mirroring your own opinion toward them'.* Does this mean that I do not respect my boss? Of course I don't! But that's because he is so rude toward me! I am sure I would change my opinion of him if he were a little more polite and appreciative! Don't quite get what Lise is getting at!

Let's move on . . .

'SECURITY, *in the true sense of the word, is the peace of mind created by the thought that there is nothing to fear, therefore, security lies in the absence of fear. Understanding this creates peace of mind, which is the ultimate outcome of security. Many people misinterpret security as having a good savings account "to fall back on", or a job with a good benefits package "just in case...", or a good stock of material possessions, or even a spouse. Real security is knowing that, no matter what happens, you have what you need inside of you to make your life work and to get her results you want. Depending on anything outside of you to provide for you, should make you feel insecure, because, ultimately, you are giving away your power.* **The only true security is within you'.**

Ok, it's a lovely concept, in principle sure. But it is so detached from the reality we live. I hate my job, but I can't quit it. If I did, how would I pay my rent? I do not feel confident enough in myself to know what to do next. Is this yet another issue I need to tackle and sort out? I have no savings, no assets, how can I be sure that I will not end up a drunk homeless person? Ok, maybe I am being a tad dramatic here, I can always count on my parents! Security . . . Just this morning a saw a quote on a Facebook post that said "Know that The Universe Has your Back". I thought it was lovely, for a brief moment it made me feel safe.... But I do I make this become part of my belief system? How To learn to feel secure in a world that is full of fear and insecurities, this is the question!

Food for thought!

'INTEGRITY, *according o Webster, means "personal honesty and independence". It also means completeness and unity. Integrity is derived from the word "Integration", in other words "as without, so within". You say what you mean in your heart. There is no "hidden agenda", no "reading between the lines". Someone who does not keep his words or does not honour his engagements, promises or duties, is being dishonest with others and, especially, with himself.*

I do see myself as a person of integrity. Ok, maybe, sometimes I say little white lies, but that's just because I don't want to hurt people. Regardless, I do not believe to have hidden agendas, I don't think you need to read between the lines with me. What you see is what you get.

Millie often tells me "Kate don't hide behind a mask', "be honest with yourself". I believe I am honest with myself I choose to show much of myself to others. And when it comes to Chris is she is full of "Kate get real" .She doesn't know him as well as I do. Speaking of which, he should be on his way soon. I will pause here Mac and put some chips in the oven. They will be done by the time he gets here. I will cook the steaks when he arrives. He likes his food piping hot. I like treating him well, he is my prince!

....

I am back, I am back

'GUIDANCE refers to the need to be of service to others. It is a return to Divine Perfection. Although we feel a need to help and guide others, we often go about it the wrong way by giving advice and making decisions for others. To guide is to share knowledge without expectation. (Millie should read this; she is always so forceful with her opinions!) *It is up to the other person to determine whether or not he will accept and utilize this knowledge. Be sure to share your knowledge only when the door is open for the other person to receive it'*

Basically she is saying that we need to mind our own business! Don't give unsolicited advice. It's not a problem for me!

And this is why I avoid confrontation, there is no point in giving my advice when the other person is set in his/hers ideas.

'He will do what he wants with it according to his own needs and his own time frame. It is your gift to him. Remember expectations come from your ego – from its need to be gratified.

'A SENSE OF PURPOSE, or a "reason for being" is vital. It provides enthusiasm and energy that propels you through your day. Are you proud of what you do for a living? Do you get excited when you talk about your work and do you feel you have a reason for being on the planet?'

Do I need to answer these questions??

'You have to feed your soul; to be creative and to tap into the pool of energy that is your very life-force. Without doing so, you will experience lethargy and anaemia – so get your blood flowing and bring yourself to life! If you are not sure what gets you really motivated, find out and DO IT!'

I love cooking for people, that's about the only thing that makes me excited. I think about the flavour combinations, the colours, the spices, it's my creative space. When it is appreciated it just fills me up with joy. Chris appreciates my food, but Jamie was/is my biggest fan. He just could not get enough. I have seen his new posts on FB and it seems so happy and so good looking! He has truly undergone a transformation and he is blossoming. It saddens me not to be part of his transformation, but I am happy for him.

Chapter 17 Exercises

>> Write down the needs of the mental body and examine the ones you have neglected in your life. In doing so, you will begin to understand the underlying dissatisfaction you feel. It is up to you to nourish your mental body. There is no way around it – these needs must be met, as they are necessary for your survival and your overall health.

I guess the mental essentials I need to pay particular attention to are: Individuality, Respect and Security. Somehow I have to understand what makes me an individual, learn to respect myself and trust in myself!

>> Determine to address each of these needs and take action. Only in doing so will you get closer to obtaining your dreams

I have no clue Lise! Perhaps I can ask my friends and family what he thinks makes me so special. My mum and Jamie always used to say that I am a very special person. I just don't feel special, so I can figure out what makes me unique?

This is a very difficult exercise for me. I am figuring thigs out. I know that Lise's words are slowly penetrating my brain and heart, they are not yet revolutionizing my world, although they are making it a much better place to be!

>> Repeat this affirmation daily:

I AM NOW DETERMINED TO RESPECT THE NEEDS OF MENTAL BODY AND THEREFORE REGAIN MY MENTAL BALANCE

Text from Chris . . . he will be here in 5 mins. Speak to you later Mac, hopefully tomorrow!!! Wish me luck

Love

Kate xxx

Wednesday 3rd June

Good afternoon Mac! It's 2pm and I am writing from home! I feel like a naughty school girl. Chris and I got quite drunk last night, and this morning we were still so drunk, he convinced me not to go to work! Funny how this happens, when the chapter I worked on yesterday was all about honesty and truth! But I don't think it is a big deal given that I don't want to be at work! It is ok to pull a sickie sometime. I don't make it a habit, do I? And have I mentioned how little I get paid? He is such an uplifting experience in my life. He opened me up to new horizons, wild sex, meat, and naughtiness. . . . maybe he is making me experience my true me? Maybe my individuality is coming out thanks to him?

Last night was great. He walked in all showered and smelling divine. He kissed me on the lips and said "what's for dinner beautiful tits, I am starving" his language is so honest, but it makes me feel desired, wanted, womanly.

He brought 2 bottles of wine, which downed with dinner and whilst watching Breaking Bad on TV.

After that he rolled a joint and starting making out on the sofa. We moved from the sofa to the bedroom and let me just say that we went on and on and on until the early hours. No way I could have gone into work today. Despite a slight sense of guilt, I feel so loved up and happy. I have managed to let go of all the crap from last week.

Chris left about 1 hour ago and I still have not managed to get out of bed! And the icing on the cake is that I got my period, so hopefully crazy has left the building.

To add to today's happy feeling, I have received an e-mail from Jamie. My heart always skips a beat when I see his name in my inbox. To think of it, it's funny how he now has this effect on me. It must be because I miss him. It never happened when we lived together! Curious . . . Maybe it is true when they say "Distance makes the heart grow fonder".

This is e-mail, sweet, sweet e-mail

"Hello my darling Kate. How are you? I am sorry I have not been in touch in a while. As you can imagine, life is pretty hectic at the moment. I love living in NYC, my course and my new circle of friends. Everybody is so positive and proactive here. I now understand why Millie says that us English lot have a deep vein of negativity running in our blood. I do miss you girls though. I think life would be complete if you were here.

I do console myself with the fact that you are happy with Chris though. And I am happy when you are. How are things with you? Any news? Are you feeling any better? In your last e-mail you sounded down?

I too have met someone, her name is Jennifer and she is a yoga teacher. She is gorgeous on the outside and on the inside. She is opening me up to a whole new way of looking at life. She is teaching me a lot about spirituality and I feel as though I have shaded my old skin and allowed my true self to come out. I hope you don't think I sound too out there? Although I have started doing this work before leaving for NYC, I now feel that I am getting in touch with my identity, I now believe more in myself and my ability to make my life the life I have always dreamed on.

I am loving my life. Here are words that I thought I would never say!

Enough about me though, what is going on with you? Let's not leave it for too long until the next e-mail. I miss you. Lots of Love, Jamie x

Ps: meaning of OM: noun, Hinduism.

a mantric word thought to be a complete expression of Brahman and interpreted as having three sounds representing Brahma or creation, Vishnu or preservation, and Siva or destruction, or as consisting of the same three sounds, representing waking, dreams, and deep sleep, along with the following silence, which is fulfilment. http://dictionary.reference.com/browse/om)'

What on earth is he talking about? Has he gone loco in NYC?

How funny though, that he is discovered his individuality when yesterday I figured out that I need to find mine? I am very happy for him, but I can't help but feel a little jealous!

I replied to him right away

'Hello my darling Jamie. How lovely it is to read your news! And to read that you are so happy and that your life is going so great! Jennifer sounds lovely, tell me more about her, maybe post some pics on FB of her? I am so pleased that you are in love too, it's amazing that we can both learn so much from our partners.

Chris and I are doing very well, we get on so well and I would be lost without him. Especially now that you and Millie are gone. I miss you both so much. He also makes my work life more bearable! You know how much I hate my job and things and not improving at all! Having Chris in the office is a true blessing. When I am stressed or upset I look at him and the world feels like a better place.

I am not sure that I am becoming spiritual too, whatever that means, but I am also doing lots of soul searching. I am reading this self help book my mum suggested "Listen to your body your best friend on Earth" and doing all the exercises at the end of each chapter. I feel like it helping me a lot, it's bringing more clarity and positivity in my life. But I would be lying if I said that all is well. I am going through some emotional upheaval too. It is bringing up so many questions in me, so many doubts and I don't what to do with them. Now that you have gone, I don't have anyone to talk to about this stuff. Chris is the Alpha male type, he does not believe in this stuff and that's fair enough.

Just the other day I read a chapter that talked about finding your own individuality and trust in your ability. I just don't know what makes me "different" from others? You remember how you always used to tell me how special I am? What made you say that? What makes me special Jamie?? Can you help me with this question?

New York sounds like an amazing place. I do miss you, but I'm very proud of you and I love you very much

Kate xxx'

I better get up Mac, have a shower and do the dishes. I am going to take this day very easy. I am meeting up with Millie for dinner later on. She wants to talk wedding, dresses in particular! That should be fun, she is so gorgeous, any dress will look spectacular on her!

....

All done Mac . . . flat is nice and tidy and I washed the smell of sex off me and my sheets.

I have a few hours yet before I meet Millie, so I am going to take advantage of this free time and share with you Chapter 18, *"Emotional Expression"*. Lise is very clever. First she ignites existential questions in you and then she gives you some tools on how to deal with the emotions brought to surface by the questions! She clearly understands people. I Love her!

'Webster defines emotions simply as "a strong feeling". These " feelings" include sadness, happiness, fear, empathy, jealousy, regret, hatred, anger, elation, joy and more. Improperly identifying or expressing any of them brings about frustration, confusion and agitation. All emotions are the result of reaction to outside stimulus. They are brought on by fear'

Here we go again, fear!! My worst enemy. Chris always tells me that I am so full of it and that I should take a chill pill. He is my guru. He completes me. What would I do without him? Here I go again with fear!

'Negative emotions drain your energy by lowering the vibration of your magnetic field. Positive emotions increase that field, through the bonding and merging that occurs in synergy with other positive fields.

That is why love heals and hatred destroys to the degree the emotion is felt'

She is so spot on, the moment I picked up this book marks the moment I became more positive. And look at what life has brought into my life. My salvation, my Chris. Yes sure Jamie and Mille are more distant now, but they are happy, and I am happy for them. I feel much stronger in myself, more in control. Some days are certainly better than others, I am still plagued by self-doubt, but that's only when I feel that my love is distant. Truth be told, it's all down to me. He does not change, I am the one who is full of paranoia and make up all these stories in my head. Must remember Kate "take a chill pill" ☺ <3

Lise carries on explaining her method to expressing emotions. (I am excited; this is really helpful!) She believes that emotions must be expressed as if they are not addressed *"The same external stimulus will continue to test you until you no longer react". "How many emotional situations have recurred in your life since your childhood because you were not equipped to express yourself correctly?'*

Don't get me started! It makes me sad, angry and resentful toward my mum. And I have decided to forgive her so what is the point of going over this again? Block it out Kate, move on.

'Meanwhile, your emotions are repressed and some of the following common behaviours are engaged to pacify yourself:

eating or drinking for emotional comfort

taking medication to calm yourself

sitting in front of the television set to distract yourself

or taking a warm bath to relax etc,'

ha! I tick all the boxes!

'When you are angry, it is not of any benefit to pretend you are not. Some people sit and think about it, waiting for "just the right time" to clear the situation up, others smoke or drink, cry, work, do housework, handiwork, or simply refuse to talk.' Did Lise write this book for me?? That's what I do, minus the smoking, I have stopped smoking a while ago.

'All of these behaviours are meant to distract you or help you ignore what you are feeling. Some people take a more active approach by engaging in a violent sport or choosing to become malicious directly or indirectly toward the other person. Pretending it doesn't bother you is a critical mistake.'

Chris likes his Cross Fit and boxing training very much. It is simply brutal (to me). But he loves it, he says it helps him release frustration! You see Mac! He is in touch with emotions, very mature my Chris.

'Another very common reaction is to "dump" on a third party'. I know what you are thinking right now! This is part of being a human being, we have friends who we can tell everything and literally dump our shit on them. But it's reciprocal. I think this is what friends are for?

Hold on, she is always ready with an answer to my question. *'To discuss your problems for the sole purpose of feeling better afterwards is called "dumping". To share something, on the other hand, even something unpleasant, with the intention of finding a solution of bringing about change, is a healthy process'.*

Got it? That's what I do with Millie and Jamie, although sometimes we don't get to a solution. Whilst I never talk much about my problems with Chris. I fear (famous word!) that he might find me boring and I don't want to put him off. After all men don't like when women moan, they don't find them sexy. I believe that the secret to long lasting relationship is to keep your man happy, is to cook, smile, be sexy and be happy. And if I am not happy, well I pretend to be. Fake it until you make it ☺. Problems are to be shared with your friends. I wish Mum had followed this rule. I think that's why my dad is so quiet. She is always sharing, talking, expressing, I think he is full of her crap and that's why he spends so much time on the golf course or with his dogs! I am not going to make the same mistakes she made. I want to make my man happy! I am not sure if my dad is a happy man or not, my parents have been through many, many ups and downs, but are still together …so… mmm …

#confusedagain.com!

Lise's steps to address emotions:

'STEP ONE: *Identify the emotion. It is important to know EXACTLY what you are feeling – is it anger, disappointment, frustration, sadness, fear, anxiety, aggression, hatred? Some of these feel quite similar. Identify it clearly. Note that two or more emotions can surface simultaneously.*

STEP TWO: *Accept RESPONSIBILITY for your response. Understand completely that you have chosen to feel this particular emotion. No one "made you feel this way". You have allowed yourself to be affected by an external factor. To take responsibility for your emotion may be difficult to do in the heat of the moment, initially, but is a critical step. Mostly, it is the ego that is having the difficulty. In order to do so, you will have to learn to step back and be objective about what you are feeling... All emotions stem from the same source – the mind. They are NEVER CAUSED BY SOMEONE ELSE! YOU ARE SOLELY RESPONSIBLE FOR YOUR EMOTIONS!'*

Ok then, so when Stephanie looks at me from head to toe and smirks, I am the one that causes me to feel bad? How can this be?

Once you understand that you always reap what you sow, you will have a different attitude about a given situation. If, for example, you experience a similar situation in your own life, accept responsibility, rather than allowing his attitude to upset you. <u>You may begin to realize that you, too, are very critical of him</u>'

I guess it could be true . . . I do bitch about her a lot too and let's face it, sometimes what I think of her is not very nice at all. "French trollop, get your filthy manicured paws off my man" is not that nice either, is it? One could argue that she deserves it, but that would mean that I do not accept responsibility for how I feel!

I don't question Lise at all, but I do think that the taking responsibility concept is a very difficult one to take. Nonetheless, I will work on it. After all even Lise says that 'Emotional Mastery requires commitment and perseverance. I don't know of anyone who has completely overcome this problem.'

'STEP THREE: Express yourself clearly and concisely to the person concerned. You may not feel this step is necessary if you have accepted full responsibility with all your heart, but I suggest that you attempt it anyway. Once you are secure in accepting full responsibility for your reaction, you have nothing to lose by discussing the occurrence with the person concerned. This will confirm that you have understood your responsibility with the heart and not with the mind.'

'Once you relax and accept responsibility for your own peace of mind, nothing is so intensely important anymore. Even if you disagree with something, it just won't affect you any longer. What a relief!

What a relief indeed . . . Here are the exercises for this chapter. I think I will have to do them tomorrow as I need to get ready for my dinner with Millie.

>> *Go through the process of expressing one emotion to someone else. You may choose to deal with one that you have been dragging around with you, to deal with one you are currently facing, or wait until a new one crops up. Believe me, a new one will crop up shortly. Be sure to express your emotion to this person AFTER you have taken responsibility for it. Acknowledge that you did not know how to love properly at the time.*

>> *Practice the three steps in this chapter until you fully understand the process. You will enjoy a wonderful sense of well-being. You will see that it all comes back to the same thing: accept that love underlines every word and deed*

>> *Experiencing emotions indicates that you feel threatened in some way. Once you learn to live from the heart, to look through the eyes of love, you will master your emotions and they will never get the better of you again. You will automatically understand what lies behind the behaviour of others.*

>> *Here is the affirmation. Repeat it with sincerity until you feel it in your heart*

I ACCEPT ALL OF MY EMOTIONS AND I KNOW I HAVE THE POWER TO MASTER THEM BY ACCEPTING FULL

RESPONSIBILTY FOR THEM. I NOW COMMUNICATE AND EXPRESS THEM FREELY.

Hi Mac, it's me, again

I am very proud of myself! I stood up to Millie!

We went to our favourite Thai restaurant and we talked a lot about her wedding, dress, venue, menu . . . her ideas are all so great, she has wonderful taste. Then the conversation took another turn.

Mille: How are you and Chris doing?

Me: Lovely, we are very close. He is so supportive of me and makes days at the office more bearable

Millie: He is very good looking. I am happy for you though last time we met I sensed that you were a bit lonely. You know with Jamie and I moving out.

Me: I am not going to lie to you Millie, I do feel lonely at times, I do miss living with you guys. But I am happy for you both. Jamie seems to have turned into this amazing young man. You know he now has a girlfriend?

Millie: I know, I saw pictures on Facebook, she is very pretty and he just looks so handsome. I have never realized that underneath the bad skin, puffy face and bloated belly was hiding such good looks!

And speaking of which . . . you also have lost so much weight, you are looking a little skinny. Are you looking after yourself? Are you eating enough?

Me: that's nice of you to say that, I do like the way I look now much more. I am definitely looking after myself. I do much more exercise and don't overeat anymore. I don't think I am too skinny; I am actually size 10. You know when they say, "Love is all you need", well it is so true. Since getting together with Chris, I no longer feel the need to overeat, I am full. Chris fills my life. He is so great for me

Millie: wow, he seems to be perfect! Is he though?

Me: what do you mean?

Millie: Honey, I tell you this because you are my best friend, but when I met him I did not get such great energy from him and he has never made an effort to get to know me and Marco. Your closest friends. He hasn't invited you to his best friend's wedding and from what I gather he hasn't really involved you in his life. Don't get upset please, I am just telling you this because I love you. You are such a wonderful, talented and generous young woman, a little naïve, when it comes to men … and I want to protect you.

Mac, I felt really hurt and attacked, what does she know about my relationship? What does she know about Chris? Who is she to judge? But then Lise's words came to mind and I remembered to take responsibility for my emotions. Millie is my best friend and although she is very opinionated and sometimes too straight forward, she does Love me. Her words come from her heart and so I forgave her. The moment I decided to forgive her I felt so much better, calmer, in control.

Me: I know you love me Mils, and I thank you for being concerned. I get your points, but he does make me happy and so I forgive him all of that stuff. You know he is your typical lad, they can only focus on one thing at a time. He is very stressed at work and his best friend and groom to be is having cold feet. I know He will involve me more in his life when he is ready. I don't think it is a bad thing to keep our relationship a secret at work. It's none of their business. My boss is a nasty piece of ..., imagine if he found out? He might ridicule me in front of the whole office!

Millie: Fair enough, just make sure that you are not just giving and giving and that your needs are met. You are such a caring person and I don't want anyone to take advantage of your good nature.

She gave me a hug and said I love you

I then took the conversation back to her wedding

If felt good to be assertive! You see Mac, I am improving!

I love you

Kate xxx

Thursday 4ᵗʰ June

4 am

I can't sleep . . . Millie's words came back to haunt me all night

I wonder if she has a point? Am I naive? Am I a fool? Who is she to judge? All relationships are different, right? Relationships, friendships, emotions, are not easy to manage. I was really hoping that Chris would text me last night, I thought, if he texts it shows that he cares, that he has been thinking of me. Take a chill pill Kate, I keep repeating myself. I feel like I am going nuts, my eyes are swelling up with tears and my heart is aching. Why do I feel so anxious? What is wrong with me? I am seriously wondering if I need antidepressants!

Oh thank God, e-mail from Jamie just popped up

'Hi Kate, darling

Your last e-mail fills me with sadness and confusion. You don't know what makes you special and separates you from the rest?

Where do I begin? You are a gorgeous young woman! You are beautiful inside and outside. Glossy dark long hair, big deep and warm hazelnut eyes, lips that any guy would want to kiss. Knock out body (I know very American!)! But above all, you are the most caring person I have ever met, you have so much love in you, so much love for others and not much for yourself! Beautiful, loyal, clever, witty and amazing cook! YOUR CAKES ARE THE BEST!

Do you honestly not see that when you look into the mirror? I have always seen it, Millie has always seen it and my friends in London have always seen it!

Darling Kate, I urge you to look into the mirror, look into your eyes and start to see yourself!

I love you so much and I want you to love yourself as much I do!

I have to go now; I am going to Jennifer's yoga class. But I am thinking of you

Jamie x'

AND NOW I AM CRYING!

....

7pm

Hi Mac

Sorry about this morning, what a drama queen ☺

I felt a little better when I got into this office to find an e-mail from Chris:

'good morning sexy, you look gorgeous today, fancy grabbing some lunch? 12.30? need to chat to you about tomorrow'

Me: 'Good morning handsome, lunch is good, I can make dinner tonight if you like, we will have more time to chat'

Chris: 'I am playing football with the lads and we are off to the pub after.'

Me: 'Fun, see you in Pret for 12.30'

My heart was pounding, he also called me gorgeous . . . Hello! I still cannot believe it!! Friday he has his interview for the Finance manager position and we have been prepping for his interview. I guess I am not just a pretty face! He values my opinion!

So we meet in Pret at 12.30, naturally we didn't go together as w/(h)e don't want the office to know about our relationship, it could complicate things. I frankly don't care but Chris cares for my reputation and he was the one to set this rule for us.

He was there already, got a table and 2 chicken salads for us. I love it that he orders for me, he is such an Alpha male! Jamie and Chris are so different, Jamie is not at all Alpha ... but I think I prefer my man to take charge!

Me: thank you for the salad

Chris: No worries

Me: what did you do yesterday when you left my place?

Chris: Why do you want to know?

Me: oh it's just to make conversation, don't worry I am not checking up on you or anything.

Chris: right yeah, went to the gym and then met some friends for dinner and a few drinks

Me: that's nice

Chris: nothing special, but listen, do you have any other tips for me for tomorrow? Do you know who will interview me?

Me: Anna the Finance director will interview you, but the job is yours! I will be there and I have provided her with all the questions. Here they are, I have printed them off for you. Anna and I get on really well and she really trusts my opinion, trust me, you are in safe hands!

Chris: wow, sleeping with the HR Manager has its perks – and he winked the sexiest wink at me!

He quickly finished his salad picked up the print out and went back to the office

'Thank you sexy, I will text you later'

Sure I would have preferred for him to kiss me and for us to walk back to the office together, but it is also quite romantic to keep things a secret, vey Romeo and Juliet. I wonder if he has any plans for my birthday? He must do, he just keeping it all a secret and he probably wants to get this interview out of the way. I wonder if I should organize something? No, I will wait for him. I have a feeling he is going to surprise me this weekend!

I walked back to the office with head in the clouds, just thinking of how hot he is and that he is my boyfriend. But I was still feeling anxious and yet again I was in the grip of fear. Millie's questions came back to me. Does he really love me? Is he using me? Why would Millie think so little of Chris and me? I don't know if I am reading to much into things, but earlier on he seemed all business, maybe is anxious about the interview, and that's very understandable. I should be more supportive!

When I got home I went for run a followed by a hot bath. And as I have nothing better to do with myself today I am going to read Chapter 19 titled . . . drum roll "Fear and Guilt"!!!! Incredible! She is in my head . . .

'Fear like all emotions is generated in the mind. Like truth, it is highly individual- what you fear may not be what some else fears. Some people

have fewer fears than others. They are called "brave". Others manage to overcome existing fears. … It is important that you are aware of your fear so that you can determine whether or not it has justification. If your physical body is in danger, your fear is justified. Your body produces just the right amount of adrenaline required to face the given situation. How many times have you experienced fear over the past few months? Was your life really endangered? Was you fear real or imagined?'

Fear of Chris dumping me, fear of losing my job, fear of getting fat, fear of not being good enough, fear of not having enough money, fear of being alone . . . should I really carry on?? I do realize that these fears are not endangering my physical life, but they feel very real to me, they make me feel anxious, depressed and lethargic. I sometimes struggle to motivate myself out of bed, struggle to motivate to go for a run, struggle to motivate myself to stay on a diet. Chris is what keeps me going, he is my motivation, he is my everything! Or is it the fear of losing him that motivates me?

'Recurring fears are the result of programming, or "imprinting" by your parents – perhaps as far back as your early childhood, or even before you were born. 'Thank you Mum, as always she is to blame for something! *'Overprotective parents unconsciously produce fear in their children'.* All I can remember is that I was more neglected than overprotected! She was too busy protecting the planet and the animals and my dad was too busy with his dogs, business and golf! But I don't blame him really, he provided such a great lifestyle for our family, my Mum on the other hand … well, what's the point of bringing up the past, I have made my peace with her now. I just have to let it go.

'However common this habitual fear-based behaviour is; it is not natural. As already discussed in this book, a person forms an image

in his mind called an "elemental", which is fed unconsciously through thoughts and behaviour that eventually cause it to materialise. **REMEMBER: YOU ARE CONSTANTLY CREATING YOUR OWN REALITY!'**

MUST REMMEBER NOT TO THINK THAT CHIRS WILL DUMP ME!

'Becoming conscious of what you are feeling or fearing will diffuse the energy that you would otherwise be channelling into making it happen. Through increased awareness and simples acts of love, you will be able to take a detached, objective look at your fears as they surface, without becoming emotionally attached to them. Thus, you will be in a position to master them'. This is good news! I think I am most definitely aware of all my fears; perhaps they will not come true! Aww I hope so!

'Here's another example: Perhaps your parents left you for a period of time in unfamiliar surroundings when you were a small child. They may have taken a vacation and left you in the care of someone you didn't know or were uncomfortable with. You may have experienced strong feelings of rejection, even panic, at the possibility of never seeing your parents again. Finding the sense of rejection unbearable, you carry the fear of being rejected into your adult life. You are so afraid of rejection that you make it happen over and over. Whenever you get "too" close to someone, you unconsciously created circumstances though which you will be rejected. The child who fears rejection gets rejected at school, at home and, in later life, will feel rejected by their spouse. Until they learn to master their fear of rejection, it will continue to happen. Fears operate subtly, breeding in the subconscious, producing other fears that gradually permeate the individual and develop into full-blown phobias.'

This is so me, I really cannot remember when the feelings of rejections came about. But I do remember that as a child, I did feel like I wasn't important enough for my parents, I wasn't loveable enough for my parents to give up their engagements and spend time with me. And if my parents could not be bothered to spend time with me, how could anybody outside my family be bothered either? I don't have many friends, I am certainly not popular with the boys and frankly I struggle to stand up for myself. Jamie and Millie are my life and they are the only ones to truly love me for who I am. And now I have Chris!

FEAR IS NOT RATIONAL. *Trying to overcome it rationally will not work.* THE ONLY WAY TO DEAL WTH FEAR IS THROUGH DIRECT ACTION.

'The employee who fears his boss but wants a raise will not have a chance of getting it hiding behind his desk. The only way is to take a deep breath, knock on the boss's door, face him and speak directly about what he wants. It is a good idea, also, to mention his fear. Expressing it to others helps it become easier to master. It diffuses it and gives it an opening through which it can escape at its own rate.'

And that's why I admire and love Chris so much, he has no fear! He asks for what he wants, he doesn't create fearful stories in his head. Although I understand what Lise is saying, I have tried countless times to face my boss the nasty piece of ..., but every time I am in the same room as him, every time he speaks to me, every time I see an e-mail from him, I feel burning inside, my cheeks become bright red and I can't seem to be able to put a sentence together! And I don't understand why, he just scares me!

'Don't be afraid to admit fear! People who are trapped inside themselves and wrestling with their fears alone are perpetually tormented by them. An inner voice harasses them day and night. OPEN UP and you will see that your fears can be released slowly and easily, freeing you forever. Trying to avoid dealing with them through drugs or alcohol will only suppress them – they will return with a vengeance.

The moment you begin to feel frightened about something, ask yourself what you have to lose or to gain by submitting to the fear. If you are in the path of an oncoming track, you have much to gain by feeling fear. The fear is real and justified in case. Usually, though, fear is not advantageous and only cripples you in getting ahead. Facing and admitting your fear will give you a wonderful self-confidence that will carry over into every area of your life.'

I am sure she is right, she has been right about everything else so far, but somehow I find it too simplistic. If it were that easy psychotherapist will be out of work!

As for GUILT . . .

I often use the words "I feel guilty", but I have never really given any real thought to what I actually mean by it.

'GUILT has become almost an art form in our culture – it is used to sell air time by the telephone companies and to manipulate family members and friends. It is one of the most powerful emotions!'

'"Feeling" guilty and "being" guilty are two very different things. Being guilty is knowing that you have intentionally hurt yourself or someone else. Take a hard look at yourself. When was the last time you

INENTIONALLY did harm to anyone? My guess is that it was a long time ago, if ever. Very few people are really guilty.

I never really distinguished between feeling ad being guilty, this is an interesting point.

Intent is the key word. ... There is no need to ask for forgiveness or to feel guilty if you have done or said something unintentionally that may have hurt someone else (or yourself). If you are determined to feel guilty, your subconscious will punish you and will send you an "accident" signal. It is telling you that guilt is not beneficial to you.'

I have never, never given this a thought! That would explain why I keep bumping into things and cover my legs in bruises! I am always so fearful of hurting somebody's feelings, I most certainly don't intend to. Is it all in my head!?Bloody hell! I am CRAZY! I wonder, is it just me?

However there is something that I am guilty of . . . seeking revenge! According to Lise, when you seek revenge, *'you are guilty because you are acting consciously with the intent of bringing harm to him. You will cause an inner disturbance that will force you to admit guilt. In order to neutralize guilt, you must admit to your thoughts or actions and ask for forgiveness, from the other person or from yourself.'*

The revenge I seek is against Stephanie! I think she is hideous and treats me like a piece of shit! In my day dreams I wish I could chop her hair off and feed her grease so that she her skin bursts into spots and gets fat! But I have not really done anything to her and I certainly would not want to apologise to her for having these thoughts ☺ BITCH!

'REMEMBER: every thought is a vibration that travels out into the world and is received by the person you are thinking of, whether he is aware of it or not. Whether the thoughts are those of love, or hatred, it will reach the one from whom it was intended.'

Score! Bitch Stephanie is getting my bad vibe! Hope she wakes up with a big old spot on her chin tomorrow morning! I am sorry Lise, she deserves it!

'In order to cleanse and purify your inner self, to love unconditionally, you must learn to rid yourself of each and every emotion as it rises. When you are guilty, address it and ask for forgiveness. Do it for your own sake, regardless of how you think the other person may react. Your ego, the inner voice that undermines your growth, will say: "What if he says? ... what if he thinks of me ... what if he makes fun of me ... what if he accuses me? DON'T LISTEN.'

I will do my very best to follow Lise's instructions, but I am afraid I am not there yet, I simply dislike Bitch Stephanie! One day at a time, baby steps, I might even get there. At the moment I can't, I hate when she talks to Chris, it makes me very jealous. I guess it is the fear of losing him that makes me hate her so much. To top it all up, I hate the fact that all men seem to like her! The boys in the office literally drawl over her. The only man she didn't put a spell on is Jamie! They met at our Xmas party a couple of years ago and told me that she wasn't very nice and that he could never find somebody like her attractive. Mind you, 2 years ago, Jamie did not look as hot as he does now and she could not be bothered with him. Too much of a (I quote with a French accent) "Looser" for her! I bet she would be all over him he she saw him now!

Anyways . . . where was I? Guilt... yes, what I found very interesting is the following paragraph:

'If you break a glass while doing the dishes, how do you react? Think about it – did you break it on purpose? Perhaps just for the fun of it? Not likely. Why are you so hard on yourself? An accident is brought on by your subconscious – t is the way you punish yourself to neutralize guilt. Ask yourself what you were feeling guilty about and deal with it. Stop blaming yourself, learn to love and accept yourself and you will do the same for others easily.'

Note to self, Must pay attention to little accidents! I am forever bumping into drawers, desks, chairs, I am covered into little bruises! I am literally plagued by guilt then?! Mamma mia! Ice Cream please!

Exercises for this chapter are:

>>*Identify all of your fears. Choose to master one of them and take action, one step at a time. Do the same for all of the fears you have listed.*

Mmm . . . where do I begin?

- I am afraid Chris will dump me
- I am afraid I will lose my job
- I am afraid of getting fat
- I am afraid of being alone
- I am afraid of being poor

OK too depressing, I don't want to get down the negative spiral! I know I have to deal with these fears, take a chill pill and I will be fine. I am not a mess I am just embracing change!

>> *Make a list of the things you felt guilty about over the past three days. Beside each one, note whether you were actually guilty or whether you just " felt guilty".*

Ok, I have to come clean here! I hate a chocolate bar every day this week! I have been feeling so down. And I have come on my period! But I have made up for it with the running though!!! Do I feel bad? Yes, I feel so guilty cos I complain that I am fat and I cannot stop eating sugar!

>>*Note any accidents over the past week to determine what you were feeling guilty about at the time.*

Don't know this exercise is too difficult!

>> *Repeat the following affirmation often until the little voice in your head stops and until you stop feeling all your energy to the fears you have created. No matter how long you have felt worried, doubtful or tormented, this affirmation will apply:*

I AM THE SOLE MASTER OF MY LIFE AND ANY CONSCIENCE WITHIN ME, OTHER THAN MY OWN, IS EXPELLED AND REALESED IMMEDIATELY.

The more energy you put into this affirmation (rather than just thinking it), the more impact it will have and the faster the results. Say it out loud in front of the mirror, if need be.

In this affirmation, "another consciousness" is mentioned. I am referring to the little voices that undermine your true self – the ones that are born of insecurity and fed by fear. Refuse to listen to them any longer and they will die out. You will no longer feed them.

For the person who is wrestling with chronic fears and phobias, I strongly suggest that you say this affirmation hundreds, if not thousands, of times a day, to flush out the negative energies. After a few weeks, you will feel lighter and he battle will become easier. YOU CAN OVERCOME!

To think of it, I do feel bad about the last e-mail to Jamie, so I want to make amends:

"Hi Jamie

How are you? How is life in NYC? How are things with your new girlfriend?

I wanted to thank you so much for your last e-mail. It was very sweet. I am an ok girl, I don't think of myself as so special, but it is nice to know that others do.

All is well now, please do not worry about me… it's that time of the month and you know how I get! Chris says that I am a drama queen! I am too sensitive he says! And he is so right, I really ought to change this side of my, it's not pretty. It is very annoying!!

Nonetheless, I have now figured out why I am this way. I am plagued by fear! Today I was reading that self help book I told you about and it came very clear to me that I am incredibly fearful of life. I am literally scared of everything, but most of all of not being good enough. I am afraid of not being liked! So my new found resolution is to start loving myself, accepting who I am, the good and the bad!

And this new found resolution has created a different energy in and around me and I choose to get excited about life as opposed to anxious. And how can I not be excited about life knowing that Chris is arranging a surprise for my birthday on Saturday?!

I am excited to spend my 30th with him, but I will miss you and Millie! It'll be the first time I will be without you guys on my birthday. I have decided to distance myself from Millie a little as she seems to have so many opinions on Chris and most of them are negative. I know she is very protective of me, but right now I don't need it. I wish you were here with to restore some balance in our friendship!

I am sure she will change her mind when she sees that Chris has made more of commitment to me.

Anyhow Honey, I best be off, I miss you very much and I love you.

Kate x

Ps don't worry about me, enjoy your new fab life!'

There, I feel better now

Good night Mac!

Friday 5th June

Hi Mac!

The day before my B day and Chris got the job!

He had his interview at 10 am and he did really well. In the end my boss sat in the interview, but he was on his blackberry all the time.

So I ended up asking Chris all the questions we prepped for. At the end of it, I told my boss that Chris was perfect for the job – of course he is! - Surprisingly he murmured 'whatever you think Kate, make it happen'. I think his ex-wife is taking him to the cleaners! He is such a nasty piece of shit, he deserves it. Off the point though, so Happy that I helped Chris to get this job. He deserves it. He is so smart although I am a little biased!

After the interview he gave me the sexiest, yet sweetest wink! He knew he had nailed it. When I went back to my desk, I sent him an e-mail to tell him that he did really well and that he had the job. His replied: "Awesome! Thank you sexy", Me: "Do you fancy a celebratory drink or two tonight?" But he had already arranged to meet the boys to get and I quote "wankered" (such colourful choice of words). I will have him all to myself tomorrow! My birthday! I wonder if he got me a present?? I think he has. The other day I saw a little "Pandora" gift bag in his gym bag. My heart skipped a beat. I am so excited. I worried so much for nothing!

Anyway, lonesome me has some serious beautifying to do tonight, wax, wax, wax … ouch … no pain no gain, it will all be worth it! I have bought some super sexy yellow lingerie for tomorrow night. I want to look and feel amazing for my 30th!

But before I do inflict pain on myself, I am going to open a bottle of Pinot Grigio and tell you about chapter 20, 'Emotional Essentials'. No dinner for me tonight, I want my stomach to be flat for my birthday. Speaking of food, I have been doing very well lately, I am trying the Atkins diet – it is a lot easier to follow as a meat eater! I am almost there, almost size 8! It feels good to be slim!

'Emotional Essentials':

'To maintain optimal emotional health, there are seven fundamental needs that must be met. They are discussed here in order of importance. The more nourishment you give your emotional body, the closer you will get to mastering your emotions.

BEAUTY as seen through the inner and the outer eye, beauty that is heart-felt nourishes the soul. It calms the mind and relaxes the physical body. Beauty vibrates on a higher plane than what is ugly and mundane. ... You sense a deep feeling of peace and happiness, as if all is right with the world if only for a moment.'

This is exactly how I feel when I see Chris, he is the most gorgeous thing I have ever seen... such beauty.... and more ;)

CREATIVITY is the expression of your individuality, your essential nature. Lack of creative expression in your life will affect your well-being. If you are currently trapped in a job that is monotonous or unfulfilling, you must compensate with creative recreation until you can find a job that will inspire you. If your work requires you to be creative, you may want to balance it with a more mundane life at home.

She is right, I have got to start baking cakes, when I bake I feel good, I feel like all my problems disappear and I am totally engrossed in the moment. Unfortunately Atkins diet and cakes don't quite go hand in hand ....

'CONFIDENCE, in this context, refers to self-confidence, which is the capacity to express and reveal oneself to another without fear of being judged.'

Yeah, easier said than done! This is a hard one for me, even now that I am a slim new me!

BELONGING is defined as a sense of being "part of" something ...a group, a community, a family... it validates us and gives us a sense of order. Some people are in tune enough with the Universe to understand and acknowledge their place in it. Most of us just want to "find our place in this world". Where do we "belong"?

Good question Lise, where do I belong? With Chris that I know!

HOPE is that "light" at the end of the tunnel –Realize in your everyday life that everything turns out for the best. There is a Divine Plan, even though you may not see or understand it, there is a bigger picture. Whatever you are experiencing right now is part of your development; it is a learning experience. As you go forward and grow, there will be more light, more warmth, move love – inside you and in your life. DON'T EVER LOSE HOPE! Those who have lost hope experience depression and/or low blood pressure as their flame burns low.

I am always hopeful Lise

'AFFECTION is expressed through physical contact, words of encouragement, gifts, flowers, notes, compliments, small deeds (or large ones) or simply, a warm smile. With affection, you "affect" someone else. If you are lacking affection in your life, did you forget to sow some?'

'GOALS are critical! They give you a reason to get up in the morning – purpose. .. Without goals, the energy of your life becomes stagnant – it stops flowing because you have no place to it to go! Goals will increase the quality of your life by giving it life! Have specific goals – even grand ones. IT IS BETTER TO MISS A GREAT GOAL BY A LITTLE THAN TO ACHIEVE A SMALL ONE.'

I am well aware of the importance of goals, HR is all about goals and targets! But it never occurred to me that I should set myself some life ones! What are my goals Mac? Apart from marrying Chris, what else do I want to achieve in life? Get to a size 8, quit my job ... and what else? Could this be the reason why I have been feeling a little off lately? Not enough life goals? What are my dreams and aspirations?

I DON'T REALLY KNOW! AM I APATHETIC? OR JUST PLAIN PATHETIC?!

Here I go again, feeling sorry for myself! It might be the vino talk, I have almost gone through the bottle and I have hardly had any food today!

Exercises

>> Before continuing onto Chapter 21, take a sheet of paper and write down the needs of your emotional body

>> Determine which of these needs you have been neglecting. Which emotional nutrients do you need

>> Once you learn to meet your emotional needs and nurture your emotional body, you will begin to master your emotions and MASTER YOU LIFE!

>> Here is your affirmation:

I AM NOW DETERMINED TO RESPECT THE NEEDS OF MY EMOTIONAL BODY AND I REGAIN MY EMOTIONAL HEALTH.

I will leave the exercises for next week, I have a feeling that my weekend will be too busy ... I cannot wait to see what is inside that Pandora bag!! I will ensure to thank my love with the best sex of our lives! Yep, I am drunk!

You know what, I am going to treat myself to a beautician tomorrow. Waxing is much less painful when somebody else does it and I want a spray tan! Spray tan make you look even slimmer! And I will also book the hair dresser and get my nails done! I want to look and feel AMAZING for my 30th!

Saturday 6th June

7 am – can't sleep, I am too excited

IT'S MY BIRTHDAY TODAY!!!

Good morning Mac!

Wish me happy birthday! I am 30 today! I am so old!! But I do have the most amazing boyfriend, who is taking me out for a romantic dinner tonight! I think? It must be! I don't know where or when as it is all a big surprise. How sweet!

He is coming to pick me up at 7.30, so I have about 12 hours to make myself impossibly beautiful, find an outfit and read all my Facebook birthday wishes.

What to wear, what to wear ... I think a little black number will do just the trick! The Atkins diet and the recent emotional turmoil (totally caused by myself!) have helped my quest to the ideal size and I happy to announce that I can now fit my size 8 skinny jeans! So happy, this causes for a celebration too!

I have booked the beautician and the hairdresser (going all out here!) for 12.30 and as I have time plenty of time to kill! Coffee and Lise, what better way to start the morning! Confession Mac, I have a little bit of a headache from the vino last night, but nothing major and Lise always helps inspires me, even when I am not sure what she is going on about! And I got to the last chapter! Isn't it curious how I got to the last chapter on the day of my birthday? I would say that this is my Mum's best birthday present. I have learnt so much, feel so blessed and excited about being 30!

Chapter 21 - HARMONY AND BALANCE

'The truly spiritual being understands that others are mirrors of himself. This is a profound and extraordinary revelation that becomes the lifeline to your personal development. As you grow in your awareness of this concept, you will begin to see that the more love and beauty you see outside of yourself, the more love and beauty will be reflected with you. A sense of peace overcomes you and once you truly understand and accept that everything and everyone is "as it should be". Can you imagine what this world would be like if we could all see the God-self, the perfection, in each-other?'

I am beginning to see this, today is such an example of how my life has improved in the past month. I have lost 3 dress sizes, I love, love, love it! I have the most gorgeous boyfriend (my very own Brad Pitt) who loves me and yes I don't like my job, but I am more at peace with it! and of course I have made peace with my mum, which is also a massive thing! And let's not forget that I stood up to Millie, or sort of! I am learning to love myself more and more

To quote a famous song. "Love is in the air, everywhere I look around..."

'The smallest criticism or the slightest judgment toward an-other is a reflection of what you judge and do not accept about yourself. When you criticise or judge someone, it's as though you were saying: "I am God and the other is not". A truly spiritual person sees his own perfection, hid God-self as clearly as he sees the perfection in others. We are all manifestations of God, but we must learn to express God as a whole... The reason we are on this planet is to learn to express Divine Perfection and we will do it in our own way - our own style - at our own pace'

And here goes cookie Lise, what does she mean?! I guess it's one of those things that come to you when you least expect them, just like Chris! I still don't know what my purpose in this life is, I honestly don't. But I am sure it will come to me, maybe I will ask Chris or Jamie ... they know me so well! They all, including Millie, know what their purpose in life is. I am so jealous, but I mustn't put myself down! It's my birthday after all!

'When souls are conceived, we are each given a puzzle that was identical to the puzzle given to all. Since each of us is unique, we will put the puzzle together in our own way. Some will do it more quickly than others, some will start with the edge, some according to colour: most of us will grab what we can identify with at random. Ultimately, to complete our evolution, we must complete our puzzle.' I hope I am not too far away from completion, I cannot stand puzzles Mac! I don't have the attention span for them! They give me a headache!

'Using the mirror analogy, you begin to understand any reaction you have to what you are seeing in others because you do not accept the same thing in yourself. It strikes a chord in you because you identify with it, whether it is a behaviour or a personality trait. Your superconscious mind is giving you a signal that whatever if bothering you about someone else is something you need to identify and work on in yourself. You do not allow that part of you to be seen because at some point in your life you had decided that such a trait was unacceptable. You no longer acknowledge who you are. Once you have learned to respect yourself, you will be able to accept others. Like a mirror, seeing beauty in others is a reflection of your own inner beauty.'

As much as I get this, I don't get how Stephanie and I are similar. I hate that girl, she is a real Bitch! I am not sure how the bitch in me is the same as the bitch in her. She is one very special Bitch!! Bitch!

'So, instead of judging the behaviour of others and reacting to it, accept the fact this personality trait is in you and ask yourself what the consequences would be if you were to act the same way. What do you have to gain by behaving differently? Concentrate on your puzzle - by concerning yourself with everyone else's, you will be neglecting your own. GET IT TOGETHER! The more puzzles that are completed, the closer our world will be to perfection!'

Lise is such an optimistic bunny, I will concentrate on my puzzles, but I still don't get how Stephanie and I can possibly share things in common. Anyway, I will get my shit together and ignore her . . . enough said!

'All life forms in the entire Universe are Divine expressions of God. Every living thing has an innate understanding of Divine Law - only mankind has lost touch with this and has a need to re-learn it.

Living "in the moment" is a characteristic of the spiritually evolved human being. That becomes increasingly difficult to do as the pace of our world increases. All most of us can do is "hang on" - so many of us choose to "hang on" to the past. By hanging on to the past, you are hanging on to accumulated, outdated thoughts and possessions that drag you down and slow you down. It's like climbing a staircase, taking each stair and piling it on your shoulders as you go. What a terrible burden you place on yourself! Are you hanging onto the past? Take a look around your home. Are your closets, your drawers, your attic and your basement crammed with accumulated "stuff"? Do you hesitate to get rid of all that "stuff"? Ask yourself what you are REALLY hanging onto and learn to let it go.

Ok she got me, yet again! I am a serious hoarder! I never throw anything away as I think I might need it at some point. Everything has sentimental value and I am completely attached to my memories. My desk at work is what I call 'organised chaos', but it is chaos nonetheless. I guess I need to be brave in my 30s, new decade, new dress size (8!!!!), new me!

'While many people remain attached to the past, some think only of the future. They either worry about it or wait for things to happen to them. "When I get married, my life will be better ... when I get a house ...when I have a child . . . when I lose weight... "Life is happening NOW! You are alive NOW! BE HAPPY, BE YOURSELF - NOW and everything will come to you. Your energy must be focused on NOW in order to take action.

Learn to think in this order: 1. BEING 2.DOING 3.HAVING, instead of "having, doing and then being". If you are the type of person that says "If I could HAVE this, then I could DO that, then I would BE happy... ", you will never have, do or be anything. That way of thinking is in reverse to the necessary process. Here's an example of effective thinking "BE HAPPY, DO WHAT YOU WANT AND YOU WILL GET WHAT YOU WANT".

I cannot help but think that this book is written for me, but I also think it is over simplistic! How can I possibly leave my job, the job I hate? Without a job I cannot pay the bills, I would not be able to support myself. How can I be happy with 5 days a week I have to drag my now shrunk to a size 8 behind to the office??? I wish I could e-mail Lise a list of all my questions. For I am sure she is right, but I just cannot see what she really means.

'The New Age is only beginning - it is based on the philosophy of BEING, rather than HAVING. All those who persist in thinking that "having" is more important than "being", will continue to be unfulfilled. Getting rid of everything you won is not the answer'. phew, I thought I would have to shave my head, drop everything and become a Buddhist nun.

The answer lies in LETTING GO of your attachment to things and old ideas. LET GO AND LET GROW so that you can focus on being happy, which is NOW!'

I AM VERY HAPPY NOW!

Lise goes on suggesting meditation as a means of quieting the mind and getting in touch, communicate with the superconscious mind. She suggests 20-30 minutes, preferably early in the morning, before breakfast. She obviously has never lived in London! What? Am I supposed to wake up? 5.30 am? I am ridiculously slow in the morning, not a morning person me!

Best get ready now, the exercises will have to wait until Monday, most probably ☺

Off to get beautiful. Later Mac x

9pm . . .

Chris is not coming Mac! No birthday dinner! No celebration of any sort! He is sick! It appears that he is so sick, he forgot all about tonight! I had to text him at 8.30 pm! He even forgot to wish me happy birthday! Can't help to feel that something is up, although it can be perfectly true. He partied too hard last night and he had all the rights to do that! He says he has food poisoning, which could be very true too . . .but what about me? I am sad and disappointed. All dressed up and nowhere to go. Jamie is in New York, I have already told Millie that I was going out with Chris and I won't give her the satisfaction of telling me 'I told you so'! I feel so deflated, I was so looking forward to tonight, I never thought that I would spend my 30th birthday alone, at home, how sad! Maybe I deserve it?

I think it's Sex and the City and a bottle of wine to celebrate my 30th!

Happy Birthday to me!

Kate x

PS: I am honestly trying to apply the teachings of chapter 21.

'Don't waste your time worrying about the future. Concentrate on NOW and have faith in your own ability and the Universal Law of Abundance to ensure that you will be provided for. You become what

you think - you create your reality. Gather your resources, stand tall and find your balance. BE YOURSELF, in all your perfection, and everything will be as it should. Then you can go forward in confidence, toward your goals and the realization of your dreams.

Trust your innate divinity to guide you. Know that, when something "unpleasant" happens, that it is a necessary learning experience for you. It is a signal from your superconscious mind that you are thinking, speaking or acting in a manner contrary to the Law of Love. It is a little nudge from your God-self that helps you to keep you on track. Operate from your heart centre at all times and only god thing will happen in your life.'

I can't help but wonder, what I can possibly learn from being stood up by the man I love? On the day of my 30th Birthday? And finding myself a billy no mates? What is so wrong with me? I certainly don't feel divine, when I am being myself nothing good happens to me! I give up... I am going to get drunk all by myself on my birthday!

Sunday 7th June

Good morning Mac, or is it?

I downed 2 bottles of Pinot Grigio last night! I have splitting headache and I look and feel like shit! So much for being a manifestation of the Divine! So much or I am God and I create whatever I desire! So much for Inner Peace! I am a fuck up! But!!! My hair still looks pretty good from yesterday's blow dry! What consolation!

Why Mac? Is it because I am not good enough?

I don't deserve someone like Chris! What have I done wrong?

I could have been cooler; I could have been skinnier, obviously I am not worth the effort. Maybe I should have loved him more? I know I am not very good at showing emotions, or have I showed too much too much too soon? I should have been more French and cool like Bitch Stephanie??

Jamie sent me a sweet e-mail

'Darling Kate: Happy Birthday! You are 30 today and you are turning into the most amazing 30 year young woman. I wish you were here, but I am happy in the knowledge that you are having a fabulous time with your Chris and I hope he knows how lucky he is.

I love you lots

Jamie x'

Yes Jamie! A great time with my Chris! It's 1 pm and he hasn't even bothered to get in touch. Maybe he is still sick? I must try to be über cool, I am 30 after all! Maybe this is all in my head? Am I being too much of a drama queen? Why would he say that he loves me if it wasn't true? I now feel terribly guilty for thinking this, maybe he is very sick... Poor baby

Millie also texted me to check that I had a fab time last night! She has invited me to a spa weekend, courtesy of bank of Millie. The thing is though, I would never be able to look at her in the in the eyes after last night's fiasco! I cannot possibly accept! I will deal with that later.

Mum also called this morning. I had to make up a story of how wonderful my date with Chris was! I could not be bothered to get into the whole thing with her. She would have said that it was no excuse, I need to learn to love myself so that I can attract people who truly love me and all her psycho BS.

Lots of Facebook messages, which was very nice and even one from super Bitch Stephanie, ' Bon anniversaire Kate, hope you have a great day and night!' Bitch, she is like a black crow, she is bad luck!

Whatever, I am going back to bed for a bit as I am really not feeling so great! My head is pounding so hard from all the booze I drunk last night, on my birthday, by myself!

4 pm.

Still no text to Chris, should I send him one? He is not well after all, but yesterday was my 30th birthday!?? Is it too much to ask for a little more attention? If he truly loves me, could he have at least sent me text or two?

Do I have high expectations? Should I be more understanding? Is there something wrong with me? Or should I just chill?

I am going to have something to eat and take a warm bubble bath … I bought myself some expensive salts and aromatherapy bath gel from Neil's Yard. Lavender and Geranium to remind myself of the sweet smell of the Med!

Have I mentioned how nobody has bothered to give me any gifts? Ok Millie offered a SPA weekend and Jamie is away … no flowers no nothing from Chris …

5pm

Shower and food did the job, I have calmed down and now feel cool, calm and collected. I am going to send Chris a text:

'Hi Chris, How are you feeling? Hope you are better than yesterday. It is a shame we missed out on my birthday celebrations, but I am sure we can make up for it soon. Take care, Love, Kate x

I think it is a nice message, caring, supportive and cool!!

6pm

Text from Chris – I was beginning to lose hope! Let 's see

'Kate, I think it is time we end this relationship, I don't feel the same way anymore and I don't want to string you along. You don't need to reply to this, let's just agree to be cool.'

What the fuck! I am all cold and hot! I feel as though my world has collapsed on me, I am speechless, don't know what to say, do, or think?! What is going on?? I don't understand? There were no signs that this was coming? What did I do? I need to get some fresh air and pour myself a stiff drink before I decide how to reply to this!!! Do not reply my arse, stay cool?? How rude is he!!!! I am in a complete state of shock! And who do I call? Who do I talk this through? No bloody one! My so called friends have all deserted me! I am totally alone. I am such a fucking idiot!

8 pm

I replied, how could have I not to?

'Chris, I don't understand? This comes completely out of the blue, I thought all was good with us? I can't not reply; I think I deserve answers. Is it something I have done or said?'

I waited for a couple of hours, downed a bottle of wine by self and kept tormenting myself, going around in circles, driving myself mad. What did I do? What did I say? What happened? I can't even talk it through with anyone as I know they will rightly think that I am an idiot and tell me 'I told you so!'? I am going to be sick!

11 pm

Literally A Bombed was dropped on me, why am I such a gigantic stupid fat cow?

'If you insist I will tell you what is wrong with you! With pleasure! You are a moron! you are so gullible; you can't see when somebody is using you! Did you really think that somebody like me could possibly go out - let alone fall in love! - with somebody like you!? Did you ever stop and think? You have allowed me to use you!

You are spineless, have no personality and your tits are just about the only thing I could stand about you. I don't know how I managed to keep this act up for so long, I can't fucking stand the site of you! See you in the office, Looser!

Ps: don't bother telling people in the office, nobody would believe you and anyway, they all think you are an idiot! Apart from your fat assistant!

I texted back:

'What have I done to you to deserve this? I might be an idiot, but you are a nasty piece of shit!'

My heart is in bits and I could barely type, I have so much adrenaline running through my body

'Let's try to keep it civil in the office for appearances stakes, you wouldn't want the bosses to find out how much of an idiot you really are?'

Mac, I don't understand why this is happening to me, I thought things had got better, I thought my life got better! I lost all that weight, I helped him in his career, I have been nothing but supportive, I loved him, he said he loved me . . . was it all a lie? I don't know what to do with myself! Wine and tears are all I can do. I cannot talk to anyone about this! More than ever I feel isolated, worthless and so badly hurt. I will take some of those Kalms pills and hopefully they will knock me out. Maybe this is all a bad dream and when I wake up all will be fine again. I just don't know how I will face going into the office tomorrow!

PART 3

The Ape and the broken heart

8 am

My head is sore, my eyes are puffy and my stomach is swollen. I managed to sleep somewhat, but I was terribly agitated, kept tossing and turning. The first thing I did when I woke up was to check my message, I thought that perhaps it was all a bad dream and that maybe Chris had texted me to tell me that it was all a silly practical joke that one of his flatmates put on him. Sadly no, I am a complete fool. A fat, ugly, fool, good at nothing!

I can't face the office today; I have sent Vicky an e-mail. I have told her everything! I had to tell someone! She might be on the plus-size side, but she is so sweet and caring and nice! Looks are not everything! Chris is good looking but a total piece of shit, bastard, SOB!

I am going back to bed now, I just don't feel good, I am too sad and angry. I need to feel sorry for myself!

2pm

I just don't understand Mac! I have no more words, I keep playing our relationship over and over in my mind. I didn't see this one coming. How can it be? Why did he use me? I don't get it. I have downed more of those Kalms, but don't worry, they are completely herbal. They do calm me down, but I need something stronger. I think I have a bottle of vodka tucked somewhere around here.

5pm

After downing a bottle of vodka, I wrote an angry e-mail to Lise – which I found on her website -, she is a fucking fraud and I am a stupid moron to have read a book, that my mum, the mother of the idiot, suggested! How desperate I have been!

'Dear Lise, Your book, Listen to Your Body, is a piece of shite! I have read it, I have done all the exercises and my life actually got worse and I hit rock bottom! You are silly fantasist, that takes the piss out of people and idiots like me take you seriously. Do yourself and the world a favour, take your book off the shelves of Amazon and stick it where the sun doesn't shine. Divine my fucking arse!'

Tuesday 9th June

No Mac, I don't feel better at all. I am still in such a state of shock! Last night I collapsed as I wrote the e-mail to Lise, which I never sent by the way! Although I think I should, but what's the use? She will not reply and if she did, she will say that I have done the exercises correctly or some shit like that!

No work again this morning, I just cannot face it! Vicky is being very supportive though and this morning I found an e-mail from her. ' Hi Kate, hope you are feeling better. Chris was in the office today and he seemed to be very chirpy (B*****d!). He and Stephanie went out for lunch and when they came back they were all giggles and laughter. I think there is something going on there! Will you be coming in tomorrow? Please don't hesitate to call me if you need to chat. Lots of love Vicky'

I am so mad, fucking Bitch, fucking Stephanie! I hate her! I hate her!

But no, I am not going in today. I need a day to compose myself! No more drinking for me, I will go out for a walk, possibly run (????), go to the hairdresser, buy some new makeup. Tomorrow the plan for revenge begins! Goodbye nice Kate, hello Bitch Kate! The plan is to look impossibly good, after all I am a size 8 now! Walk into the office, ignore everyone (they all hate me after all) and start to plot! I will make everyone pay for this, I am HR Manager after all. I am going to regain my power and show them what idiots they are!

8pm

I do look much, much better Mac, but inside I am a mess! I'd better pick some clothes for tomorrow. I am thinking a tailored black suit jacket, mini skirt and pip toe shoes. All in black, so that I will look even slimmer and definitely mean! They have to take me seriously, I will make them!

Got a couple of e-mails from Jamie and texts from Millie. I just cannot bring myself to reply to them. I know what they will say and if I lie to them, they will know something is up! Thank God I have you Mac! and Vicky!

10.30 pm

I have just taken about 10 Kalms. Hopefully I will drift off in a nice sleep. I cannot go to work with puffy eyes! No more tears, he will not have my tears. I will never show him that he has broken me, that he has broken my heart! I am through with men, I am through being nice, I am through with self-help books, I am through being an idiot!

Revenge Day 1 begins tomorrow

Good night Mac

Aww Mac, I should have not gone in! Today was the most atrocious day of my life. And that's saying a lot considering all that has been going on in the past few days!

I walked into this office, looking, although not feeling, good! I said hello to everyone and with a big beaming smile. But my body language said, revenge is a dish served cold! I sat in my office, a concerned Vicky came in and closed the door behind her. She is a sweetheart that Vicky! We had a quick chat and she run me through today's meetings.

As we were talking, I see Chris walk down the corridor headed toward the kitchen. Damn glass window offices. He looked toward my direction and launched the most charming, yet hostile smile at me. Fucker! I obviously did not reply back to him and turned the other way, tossing my air. In my head I gave him two fingers and mimed, well you know what! Vicky looked at him in disdain, turned to me straight away and asked if I was ok.

My heart jumped in chest and my cheeks blushed in utter anger. I am going to have my revenge. I just don't yet know how, what and when!

At around 11, I walked into the Kitchen to make myself a coffee. Stephanie, correction, Bitch Stephanie got up from her desk and followed me.

S: 'How are you Kate', with that stupid stick up French accent!

Me: I am good Stephanie, thank you for asking

S: 'You look like you have lost weight, although your face looks puffy. But well done nonetheless.

Me: 'Oh well, thank you for noticing Stephanie. You look very good too, but then again you always do.

Sadly she does! She is a skinny size 6, long dark brown hair, always perfectly groomed and manicured. She is always effortlessly elegant, I hate her! French Bitch!

I honestly don't have anything against the French, I love France, the food the wine ... she is the only French thing I hate!

S: 'Perhaps you have been crying? Perhaps a boy hurt you? Chris maybe?

Me: I looked at her stunned 'I don't know what you mean'

She then proceeded to drop a bombshell on me

S: 'I know everything!'

I looked at her in a pure state of shock, my jaw literally dropped.

S: I know everything. And do you know how I know everything? I helped Chris set the whole thing up.

At this point, I still cannot say a word. I feel as though I am falling in a black whole of utter confusion

She carries on ...

'Chris and I are lovers! Look at us, we belong together. Are you really so clueless. Do you think that somebody like Chris would go out with you? He just needed a bit of help with his career, we want to get married next year, and you were our best way of getting there!

Adrenaline kicks in, anger kicks in, I was imploding!

'What are you saying exactly Stephanie' I don't know how I refrained from calling her with her real name, Bitch!

'Chris and me set the whole thing up as we knew that you had a crush on him. We knew you are gullible, well stupid! And would have done anything to have him and to hear him say 'I love you' to you. But he does not, it was all made up! And I know you had sex, I told him that he didn't need to go that far, but he said it was a necessary part of the plan. But he was disgusted every time he had sex with you!'

Me: 'Why are you telling me this?

S: 'Because Chris is mine and he has never been yours! You are an idiot and I despise you! And if you tell anyone, Chris will go to your boss and expose you for sexual harassment!

My eyes were filling up with tears, but I didn't want to give her the satisfaction. In my head I threw my hot coffee one her white jumpsuit and told her Fuck you, French Bitch. But I didn't, I simply left the kitchen and went straight to my office. Picked up my bag and told Vicky that I wasn't feeling well and left. I just managed to hold the tears in until the elevator. Then I just crumbled, I put on my big sunglasses and proceeded to sob my heart out.

I cannot believe that some people would be so mean and that I could be so blind not to see what was happening!!! No words can describe how I am feeling. I am broken!

Thursday 11th June

I am an idiot, I deserve it

Friday 12th June

I am an idiot, I deserve it

Saturday 13th June

I am an idiot, I deserve it

Sunday 14th June

I am an idiot, I deserve it

Monday 15th

Yes I am an idiot and I deserve it. I am she Gorilla with Cellulite! I can't stand the sight of me in the mirror. But they are the worst specimen of human beings I have ever met.

After spending the last few days popping tranquillizers, drinking gallons of Pinot Grigio, eating ice cream and pizzas, I have decided to leave everything behind and go to stay with my parents in Ibiza.

Work can stuff itself and I texted Millie that I am going to visit my parents. They can all go to hell, London I am done with you! You are nothing but grey skies and people that will not stop at nothing to get head! Fuck you Chris and fuck you Stephanie

I have no energy for revenge, I have no energy to hate them anymore, I have no energy to hate myself, I have no energy to explain what happened to Jamie and Mille, I have no energy for explanations. I just want to fall asleep in the sun and hope that I wake up being somebody else!

Tuesday 16th June

Greetings from Ibiza Mac! Still me, same old same old Kate the idiot! The fat idiot! The past few days I managed to pile quite a few pounds back on. All that alcohol, pizzas, ice cream tubs have been an utter disaster. Chris and Stephanie are right, a fat, stupid idiot.

Mum was shocked to see me and could read that all was not well with me. But I just don't have the energy to get into it with her. She will just fill me with clichés like 'he doesn't deserve you', 'it's not meant to be', and 'something better is coming your way'. Whatever!

I just need to get some sun and lick my wounds. I want to forget it all and don't want to think about anymore. It's too painful and what's the use anyway? I am obviously a looser, waste of space, and nothing will ever change for me as I was born this way!

I am going to log off for a while Mac. ..., I am just too sad and hurt and writing more about it is not going to help!

Kate x

PART 4

The Ape and Forgiveness

Hi Mac

It's been a while

I am sorry I have been out of touch for so long, I simply had nothing good to talk about. And no, I have not been partying at all, I feel like a reclusive in this beautiful Finca in the north of Ibiza. No clubs for me, just tons of sleep and sunbathing. I have not even checked my phone or e-mails in the past 2 weeks, I just feel like I want to be invisible.

Am I feeling better? No, not really. But one good thing happened this morning and I do feel more relieved for it. I talked to Mum and I think I made peace with her (in my heart of course).

She has been very sweet since my arrival, looking after me, just like you would expect a mum to be. Something that she must have learnt to do whilst I wasn't around as she never showered me with so much attention. This morning though all this fussiness made me angry and I asked her why she was being so fake!

Mum: Good morning love, how are you feeling today?

Me: same as usual, like shit

Mum: I am sorry Kate; can I do anything for you? Can I fix you some breakfast? Do you want to talk about it? Would you like to do some yoga with me? Anything you want, I am here for you

Me: Thank you Mum . . . but as I was saying these words feelings of rage were boiling up inside and I burst!

'Have you entered the competition for mother of the year?' I know very harsh

Mum: I don't understand Honey, have I done something wrong?

Me: are you kidding me Mum? It's all your fucking fault! Look at me! Look at the mess that I am, look what a looser of a daughter you have! I never asked you to be born, my life is and as always been complete and utter shit and it's all because of you!

She remained calm as I carried on:

'You put me on this planet, but you never head time for me. Dad has always been off on business and golf travels and you have always been too busy saving the world, doing your yoga, meditating and doing all your hippy crap and never been there for me! So now, you must have a read a metaphysical book on parenting and decided to try it out! You are a fake! Just leave me alone, as you have always done'

At this point I was crying and I felt even more hopeless and lonely.

Mum started crying, she came toward me, I stepped away, she grabbed me and she gave me the warmest, tightest, loveliest hug. She said 'Forgive me, I obviously failed you. I failed to show you how much I love you, I failed to tell you that you are the best thing that I have done in my life. That you are the best creation, that I am proud of you. That I love you and my heart aches to see you so sad. Please forgive me! I love you so much! Give me chance to show you I can be the mum you long for and deserve!'

And we both sobbed, but it was great! I felt a huge amount of pain release, it was as though all the anger and sadness evaporated into my tears and I felt lighter! Of course I forgive her, she made mistakes, but she understood it and no, my life is not her fault. I love my Mum and I told her, which made me sob even more! I am telling you Mac, we had to mop the floor up, our tears made a little paddle on the floor. When we looked down, we both exploded into a crazy laughter. And it was so good to laugh, so good! Tears of joy ad tears of pain!

She gave me a big kiss and fixed me some breakfast.

'Honey, I know what you think about my beliefs, but there is nothing wrong with meditation, kindness and compassion. When you are ready, you can join me for some meditation and maybe something will shift in you. But there is no pressure, all has to happen when the right time is for you.'

Hesitatingly I said 'I Will give it a go, again! That book you suggested - was a pile of crap, I wanted to say, but instead I said – didn't help much, but I will give it a go Mum'. I am not sure why I agreed, maybe because I was so happy to have made peace with her. !? Maybe because I am still hopeful. Maybe because my heart has opened up a little today!

And so from tomorrow, I am going to have a go at meditation and will let you know how it goes Mac.

I love you Mac

Kate x

My status today – feeling frustrated! Although I feel a lot happier to have made up with my Mum. I love spending time with her now! She is actually quite cool, she has so many stories to tell, she is beautiful and how cool is it that your mum lives in Ibiza!!! I can now see what my friends see in her. Millie always told me how much she would have liked to have a mother like mine!

My first attempt at meditation sucked though!

Mum: 'Something has happened to you in London. You don't need to tell me what if you are not ready to tell me. You think that the book has not helped you. But I do believe that time has come for you to learn. So far you have read about spiritual principals, you have intellectualized the principles, but that's not enough to change your life. You need to meditate. You need to open your heart.

If you want to change, you have to be committed to change, you have to let go, let go of what is not serving you, let go of what is making you unhappy. Let go of what was and forgive yourself and others. Be open to love to come into your life, love for yourself first of all. Let go of thinking that you are not good enough!'

She takes me to her mediation room (yes she has a large mediation room!), which looks like the inside of an Indian Ashram. Incense is always burning and Balinese wooden craft works, Buddha statues and other spiritual objects ornate the walls, it is all really quite mystical. As you walk in, you do feel a certain overwhelming feeling of calmness, although I also felt rather anxious too. Story of my life! I kept thinking, 'This is not me, Kate get out, this will not work.' Something made me stay though …

... and it did not work! Sitting with my back straight in lotus position (cross legged) was just too uncomfortable. Mum led the meditation, she explained that it would have been easier for a beginner to follow words. It was nice, but I just did not get the sense of what she was talking about. Love??!! Kindness??!! Compassion??! Forgiveness . . .I could not get my head around that!

After 15 minutes, she noticed that I was very uncomfortable and fidgety so she stopped. 'You did well Kate, it's not easy at the beginning, your mind chatter, (also known in the mediation lingo 'The Monkey Mind') is too strong, but with patience and practice, you will learn to observe it and let it go. You will learn to go deep within yourself and experience peace, love, kindness, compassion and forgiveness. Trust me, it will happen. She gave me a hug and she too me to the kitchen and fixed some herbal tea.'

We drunk our tea, had something to eat and chatting some more. She gave a notebook and asked me to keep a journal of all the feelings that come up after my meditations. Now don't get jealous Mac, I took it as it is very pretty, light pink and blue with pictures of peacocks on it. But you and I have history and I am not a cheater! I will journaling through you ☺

Mum also suggested that I take 10 minutes first thing in the morning and before going to bed to write down a list of aspects, things in my life I am grateful for. She says that this exercise will help me raise my positive vibrations and it will set me up for a good day or a good night sleep.

I have literally become her spiritualisation project! But she means well and for some reason, here in Ibiza it doesn't all seem too cookie, but rather the thing you do!

I love Ibiza, we went to Benniraz beach for lunch, all vegetarian. Mum said that I am free to eat meat if it makes me feel good. 'if something makes you feel good, but truly feel good, then it is right for you'. But I am not good with that, I have changed my eating habits, as I changed many other things about myself for Chris. But I am not a meat eater, it does not sit well with me.

After lunch she took me to Ibiza town for a hot yoga class, which was crazy!!! I can't tell you how many degrees were in that studio, it felt like I was in a sauna. 90 minutes of yoga (asana practice, it's called) followed by some bizarre breathing techniques. But you know what, I feel amazing tonight, knackered, but good. I miss Chris and every time I think of London I feel like a stab in my heart, but here I feel miles away from the Kate I was a couple of days ago.

I am grateful that Mum lives in Ibiza, I am grateful that I have two wonderful friends (who I have not really kept in touch with! I hope they still love me, as I do miss them so terribly! But I don't feel ready to get in touch with them, I need to heal before I get in touch. I don't want Jamie to think that I am hopeless cause and for Millie to say, I told you so. However I have come to realise that I just cannot face to read Jamie's e-mails as I am afraid that he will tell me how blissfully happy he is with his girlfriend. I am happy for him, but I am not happy for me as on some level, I wish I was with him in New York, sharing this great experience with him. How things have changed Mac.)

And I am grateful for the sun, the water, the sun, the food that I had today and this bed, which is very inviting. So I am going to say good night Mac

Kate x

Ps I am also grateful for my making peace with my mum. I feel much better! Relieved! This is the first time I say it and really mean it, I Love Her!

Saturday 2ⁿᵈ July

It's official Mac, Mum is a spiritual Nazi! She came into my room at 7 this morning and asked me to join her in mediation. 7 am!!! She says it is best to meditate first thing in the morning before breakfast. But 7 am for me is the middle of the night!!!

It went a bit better this morning though, I managed to sit still and concentrate for over 5 minutes, I think, it is so difficult to have a sense of time when mediating.

She insisted that I write my journal. So here I am. She thought it is odd that I want to write a journal in my laptop! What's odd about that? Well I suppose she is 55! She does have an iPad though and an IPhone. Perhaps technology is spiritual too?

A whole bunch of thoughts came up, Jamie, Chris, anger, bitch Stephanie, I am hungry, I want to go back to bed.... This meditation stuff is actually quite hard work.... but I do feel calmer, I suppose that's a step forward right?

I am also supposed to do my gratitude 'assignment', but I am starving and she promised she is going to take me to a veggie café and then to the beach. Dreading it. I love the beach, but as always I am ashamed of what I look like! There will be no bikini for me! All the weight I lost, I pretty much put back on! All that hard work and for what?? I blame bitch Stephanie for this. She manipulated

Chris so well, she is … there goes the calm I managed to achieve after my mediation.

Mum is at the door, see you later Mac!

8 pm

I am so deflated Mac!

Breakfast and the beach was beautiful, but I just could not enjoy it. I felt empty and sad. Thankfully I could hide my eyes behind big black sunglasses.

Naturally Mum noticed

M: Are you ok Honey? You have gone all quiet

Me: yeah, just tired. 7 am wakeup call is far too early for me

M: are you sure? You have not said a word since we have got here. Are you going to sunbathe a little? Do you have a bikini on you?

Me; Nah, I forgot it (I lied to get her off my back!)

M: I could buy one if you'd like. They have a lovely little beach boutique behind the restaurant

Me: no thanks

M: you know darling, meditation can bring up a lot of negative and painful stuff to the surface. That's why it is good practice to write a journal. Did something come this morning? Is that why you are feeling down?

Me: Mum, look at me! Look how fat I am, look around and look at yourself, you are all so bloody beautiful and slim. Look at me. (my eyes started welling up)

M: I don't see what you see! You are not fat, you are not ugly, you are gorgeous inside and outside, when will you stop giving yourself such a hard time? When will you see what I see? When will you start to love yourself and drop all the nonsense you are convinced of?

Me: you are my mum, that's why you see me gorgeous! I look like one of the characters off the film 'Planet of the apes' and on top of that I am fat! A Gorilla! A big monkey with cellulite!

She could not say anything ... she just looked very sad

I was getting angrier and angrier ...

Do you really want to know what happened back in London? Are you ready to hear how much of I fool I am! I was taken for a ride by some colleagues at work. They identified a total clueless moron, me! This guy called Chris, totally out of my league, there was my clue! Pretended to fall in love with me to get ahead in the company. And his French girlfriend, bitch Stephanie was the master mind behind it all.

M: What? What kind of people do stuff like that? That's awful Honey, but it is not your fault

Me: of course it is, I am an idiot. How would a Brad Pitt lookalike want to have anything with me? Look at me! I am a mess, ugly fat mess!

Mum reached for me and gave me the tightest hug I have ever had. I was rigid, I was holding the tears, but she would not let go. In the end I let it go, I let go of the tension, I let the tears go. And flooding they came! There I was sobbing my heart out, letting go of a lot of crap! Letting go ...

She then said. Listen to me, trust me. You have got to stop this torture, you have got to stop being so unkind to yourself. You have got to start learning to appreciate yourself and see the beauty in you. You have to start my darling to forgive yourself. Forgive yourself for all that has been and move on. Trust me, you will feel better. You cannot carry on like this!

I just could not say anything ... had I been back in London I would have reached for the vodka and the ice cream, but instead, Mum took me home and we lounged by the pool. (yes she has a pool!) She offered to make me some food, but I wasn't hungry. I just wanted to go to sleep. Misery and negativity take a lot out of you!

f you. I agree with Lise on this one. I began to re-think about the book and how maybe I didn't get it, how maybe I skimmed over it?

Sunday 3rd July

I think, maybe some shifts are happening Mac. I was so exhausted yesterday, I slept solidly for 12 hours, just what the doctors ordered. I woke up with a much more positive spirit. Walked to the kitchen for some breakfast and for the first time I saw my mother! She was at the kitchen sink, peeling some fruit enveloped in the sunlight that was coming through the large windows. She was a mirage of a goddess. Somewhere in my heart, I finally saw my mother. Simply stunning.

She welcomed me with a warm and kind hearted smile. We had a little chat and she offered me some breakfast.

Breakfast had to wait, I asked her if we could do some meditation together. Of course, she smiled, not at all surprised as I was!

This time Mac, something happened. We followed the 'Love and Kindness' Buddhist meditation, just like we did the previous mornings. However this time, I felt different, I felt this warmth developing in my chest, a sense of protection, a sense of calm, a sense of peace, a sense of forgiveness.

My mind was finally calm, calm like the beautiful Mediterranean Sea on a warm June day. I have never felt this way before. It was amazing, you could say I was Blissed out!

At the end of the meditation, Mum asked me how it went, and I the tears came flooding again. Only this time they were tears of joy, utter joy. I felt as though my heart was unlocked and I saw everything clearly.

Me: You were right, I have to forgive and I have to open my heart. I am not sure what happened exactly, but it came clear that I am a beautiful person worthy of my love and the love of others. And I forgive all that I have attracted to my life and the way I have allowed them to treat me. Chris and Stephanie were only the manifestations of the self -hatred in me. I forgive them, they wronged me but I forgive them so that I can move on and I can let go. I forgive you Mum because you acted from a place of love and although you made mistakes with me, I know you love me. And I love you. I love you as I love my friends, who I miss dearly. My friends who I have pushed away, who love me just as I am. I see everything clearly. I can see how the book was of value. I can see that although I read it and sort of did the exercise, I wasn't present or maybe I wasn't ready. I just read it, but I didn't really own it, felt it, parciced it in my day to day life.

And I am grateful to you, to Chris, to Stephanie, Jamie, Millie, my boss, Lise, I am grateful because without all of you I would not be here, right now, feeling this sense of peace. Thank you.

I have so much more to learn about myself and want to read the book again, only now, I want to discuss it with you as you have so much to teach me and I want to learn from you.

I am no longer afraid of being me!'

I reached to her, and this time I gave here the biggest hug and all was right.

After breakfast, I felt a sudden urge to write to both Millie and Jamie

'To my darling Millie, I am so, so sorry that I have been so distant and have not been in touch in such a long time. A lot has gone on and through negative events, which I felt ashamed of telling you about, I finally found my way out and back home. I am in Ibiza now, enjoying Mum's wisdom, she is truly awesome. As you always said to me! I will one day tell you all about it, but for now I just wanted to tell you that I am sorry and that I love you.

I am not sure if and when I will come back to London, I need to stay here for now, I have a lot of stuff to work through, but I will keep in touch and I will certainly help you arrange your wedding. It will be a lot easier now that I am on site, right ☺

I have not been a good friend to you Millie, but if you let me make it up to you I will show you how much I care for you.

I love you very much

Kate x'

'To my gorgeous friend Jamie

I am still alive and I am sorry, I have not replied to your e-mails and messages. I was in a bad way, too far down in the dumps. I did not want to hear from you, I was jealous of you. Your brand new life in New York, your new found confidence, your girlfriend . . . I have not been a good friend to you.

But I know you know that I only acted this was as I was utterly unhappy, so much shit happened since you left and I felt alone and just kept falling down this whole of self –hatred and fear.

Despite reading the wonderful self help book, listen to Your body, I was not helping myself at all. And I blamed you and Millie for leaving me behind. You both had moved on and I was still stuck in a dark rut in London.

But I have left London behind and all that was. I am in Ibiza, spending time with my wise Mum. I am changing and I am seeing the error of my way. I have started to see things more clearly. I now see the light in front of me.

And to my surprise, as I write these words, (I had no idea before I started to write) I love you. You are my soulmate, and I want the best for you. I never told you what a gorgeous man you have become, attractive, kind, generous, understanding, good listener and bloody good looking!!!

Yeah sure I wish I was the one for you, but I am happy if you are happy with your girlfriend. I just wanted to tell you and hope that you will still see me as your friend and that you can forgive me.

I love you Jamie

Kate x'

I cannot believe the day I had, it is as though today is the first day of my life. I cannot believe that I have actually written to Jamie that I love him and that I find him attractive! I never thought of him that way! I have always loved him as a friend, but now I know that my love for him is of a different kind! I honestly did not see that one coming!

But as Mum said this morning, wonderful things happen when you open your heart, I guess that's what happened to me today.

PART 5

The metamorphosis of the Ape

A year later ...

Kate's life has change dramatically since we last heard from her.

Today is Millie's wedding day! She was so happy to receive Kate's e-mail and discover that her friend had finally woken up and saw herself for the wonderful young woman she was. Millie had always dreamed of getting married in Ibiza and Sofia's (Kate's mother) finca was the perfect the place! It was going to be a very intimate, stylish yet down to earth ceremony. The bride and the groom look happy and very beautiful in their white wedding attire.

Kate has been on a joyful journey of self- discovery and now feels connected to the world, she now feels that it is her birth right to be happy. Through her practice of forgiveness, gratitude and mindfulness she has made peace with the past, learnt to live in the present moment, where she discovered peace dwells! She now has positive expectation for what the future will be.

She also realised that cooking and baking is what she absolutely loves. The Kitchen is her meditation pillow, through her cooking she feels accomplished, fulfilled, everything make sense. With the help of her mum she is now setting up her first health food café' in Evissa (Ibiza Town). She has also made the most beautiful wedding cake for her best friend Millie!

But I bet you are dying to know what happened to Jamie??

This is Jamie's reply to Kate's e-mail:

'My darling Kate

I was so worried, I did not hear from you for so long! But I am very happy to hear that you have now reached the place of peace and appreciation for who you are and for the people in your life. I am also glad you can now see Sofia as we do. She is a gorgeous woman and you are so much like her! I have never told you this as I knew it wasn't what you wanted to hear, but I can now!

I have always loved you and I have always known that one day, you would wake up and see how special you are. You are so special to me. So beautiful.

I have always wanted more from our relationship, but I never had the confidence to tell you. I never felt good enough for you. And then you hooked up with Chris (a Brad Pitt look alike) and I did not feel there would be any chance.

And as the theme of this e-mail is confessions … here is how my journey of self develoemtYou once left the book 'Listen to Your Body' on the coffee table in the sitting room and I started reading it. I got my own copy as it spoke to me and it did help me to radically change my life. It led me to my own journey of self- development, it led me to yoga, my photography course, my life in NYC and my girlfriend.

Your e-mail came to me as bombshell and to be quite frank, I just don't how to respond to the fact that you Love me. I love you too, but I do have a girlfriend now and I have now landed an apprenticeship that will start as soon as my course ends.

I need some time to think. I just wish that your e-mail had come sooner, things are complicated right now.

I love you very much beautiful friend.

Jamie x'

Kate was very disappointed by this reply, but she understood Jamie's motives. She was heart-broken and immersed herself in healing herself, her body and work on her business venture.

··· ··· ··· ··· ··· ··· ··· ··· ··· ··· ··· ··· ··· ··· ··· ··· ··· ··· ··· ···

Saturday 14th October

Hi Mac!

Love is in the air *** Love*** Love***

Millie's wedding was so beautiful, she was gorgeous, Marco was gorgeous! They both wore white, they were bare feet, so simple, so stylish! The ceremony (led by my gorgeous Mum) was amazing and what followed was the icing on the cake – even better than the wedding cake that I made for the wedding – which BTW went down very well!

A total success! Although … the wedding was not the best of the day for me!

Jamie came to the wedding!!!!

After the fiasco e-mail exchange, I thought I'd give him space and we stopped all conversation. Until today! Millie had invited him to the wedding, but she wasn't sure if he was going to come. But he did

When I saw him, my heart literally skipped a beat. Mixed emotions of joy and confusion. Joy to see him and confusion of how to act. I was a bundle of nerves, but I welcomed him with a big hug.

He looked even better than I remembered. Tall, broad shoulders, warm brown eyes, and an air of quiet self- confidence.

Me: Oh My God Jamie, What a wonderful surprise, we were not sure if you were going to make it! How are you? Are you alone? Is Your girlfriend with you?

Jamie gave me the hugest and warmest and divine smelling HUG: Hi Kate, it's just me, how are you?

Me: I am well, busy, busy getting this show on the road.

And then I called Millie as I was too stunned to talk . . .

Millie: Oh My God, Jamie, you made it . . . it's so wonderful to see you. We were not quite sure if you were coming, but are happy to see you. Aren't we Kate! Give me a hug.

Jamie: I would not have missed it for the world, but I was wondering if Kate can spare a few minutes? I know you are very busy, but there is something I would like to talk to you about.

More mixed emotions, anxiety, dry mouth, heart pounding, sweaty palms... you name it! I was curious to hear what he had to say, but

I was scared of what he might say. I didn't want to spoil my day, so I said:

Can we please leave it to later? We have so many things to do

Jamie: Sure, it can wait, don't worry. Is there anything I can do to help?

Millie sensed my panic and removed him from the situation and took him to see my mum!

I could not make eye contact during the whole ceremony, I was too scared and I was literally hiding behind Mum's dress! She reassured me, she told me that he was here for me, I was too afraid of getting by heart broken. After all the work I have done in the past year to feel good, I didn't think I was strong enough for more heartbreak!

But! He caught up with me. He found me at the bar and although I was still hiding behind my mum, he asked her if we could chat!

Dry mouth, panic, shaking hands and all the rest, basically I got my knickers in a twist!

J: Kate, it is good to see you, you look great!

Me: thank you (shaky voice), you look pretty amazing too! I can barely recognize you! New York and love must do you well! How is Jennifer by the way, why is she not here?

J: we split up about 6 months ago

Me: fireworks of joy lighting up behind my eyes! – I am sorry about that (ha, not true!)

J: she was an amazing girl and taught loads, but she is not the one!

Me: I see

J: I want to apologise to you. The e-mail you sent me last year came as a shock to me. I never thought that you could love me, well you know romantically! I knew we loved each other as friends.

Me: I know Jamie, you don't need to explain, why don't we just have a drink and forget the whole thing?

J: No wait Kate, what are you talking about? I came all the way to tell you that I love you too and I want to be with you! Have your feelings for me changed?

Me: my heart burst in my chest out of utter joy! Fireworks and rose petals in the sky! – Of course not, I love you more than ever! I had given up on the idea of us being together! Then you came through the doors, looking like, quite frankly, a movie start and I did not know where to hide! I was in shock and I still am! How did you get so HOT?

Jamie took me into his arms and kissed me! Fireworks were now exploding everywhere, what a kiss that was! Warm, sweet, love filled kissed! How can I describe it, imagine you are a chocaholic and you have not had chocolate for a month … you take your first bite after such a long and time and yeah … that amazing, you feeling like you have died and gone to heaven!

We spent the most beautiful evening together, I was floating, I was too happy for words, could not stop smiling. The best night of my life!

LOVE is the purpose of life! What else Mac??

Hi Mac

I don't know what today will bring, all I know is that today I am at peace. Life just seems to be getting better and better, I feel enveloped by the warmth of a radiant light and all I want to is for everyone it to feel this way. To feel that life is a miracle and that if we connect to the spirit to find ourselves, to find guidance, to find our own truth, we can all live a miraculous life.

Life is full of waives, ups and down, but if we commit to positive expectations and trust that the Universe has your back, we can ride the waves.

Lise's book was a great starting point in my self- exploration, but it was just a concept. I was still in my head; I was not owning it. Through mediation and mindfulness, I started to really connect with myself and open my heart. I began to understand myself better, I learned to treat myself with compassion and kindness, I began to truly experience self-love rather than conceptualize it mentally. I began to release the fear.

I now truly believe that Love is our purpose in this life. .True love is freedom and joy. It is a process of intimate liberation. Love is not an obsession. Love is not a possession or the pursuit of possessing any one person or people.

My low self esteem led me to compare myself to others, put myself down and live a life of denial. I was a victim of circumstance brought about by my mind-set! I thought that if I lost the weight and I found true love, my prince charming, all will be settled, I would find happiness and acceptance for myself. I thought that if I could get a better job, I could have had more sense and meaning in my life. But even when I was in a relationship (fake!) with the boy I really wanted (thought I did) I did not find that contentment and peace. I was more troubled. I felt detached from me and everyone around me. I felt deeply alone and desperate.

I had to hit rock bottom, I had to fall deep down in the spiral of self misery, before I could see a little light. Before I could see my mother, before I could see the truth.

Real intimacy and connection begins internally. When we seek for our happiness, our acceptance, and contentment from outside ourselves we will never be satisfied. The journey starts with the first step of moving toward ourselves.

To get to where I now am, it took a radical amount of forgiveness to do. I had to foremost forgive myself for treating myself the way I did for so many years, for not seeing my true beauty, my true self. I had to forgive all the people in my life, to finally understand that they all served the purpose of leading me to where I am today.

Forgive, Love, meditate and be mindful Mac, it will all work itself out!

As to finding romance, well, what can I say? I am the luckiest girl on the planet! I have the love of most gorgeous man on the planet, Jamie!! He is my cherry on the cake! And although I now understand that my happiness does not depend on him, I could not ask for more in this life time. He is the best and I feel like I walk on sunshine when I am with him.

So much as changed in a year and if it has for me it can change for everyone. I now know what it means to be in love with life, to be in love with myself. I might be hairy, carry a few extra pounds have a cellulite, but I am the most beautiful Gorilla with Cellulite!

Enough with the spiritual chat, let's get back to the physical realm, I am off to spend a day with Jamie, I have a feeling it is going to be a magical one!

Love

Kate

x